BREATHE

NEW YORK TIM  *OR*

Car

Fall in love with the Wards

From troubled teen to successful general contractor, Jake Nichols turned his life around from his time in foster care. Divorced and single, he juggles his time between his daughter and his work. Next on his agenda, a new project that is his chance to prove his worth at the job he loves. Except he never anticipates that the only girl he's ever loved and lost as a teen is now a grown and beautiful woman in charge of the project.

Phoebe Ward has survived and conquered a painful past that includes foster care and becoming a teenaged mom. She wants nothing more than to focus on the present but it's hard when she looks into the eyes of her son, knowing she's tried and failed to find his father. She's resigned herself to raising him alone with the help of her family... Until a client meeting brings her face to face with her first love. A boy... now a sexy man she thought she'd never see again ... and the father of her child.

So many years have gone by and both of their lives have changed drastically. Will they be able to put the past behind them and find the second chance they both deserve?

Chapter One

PHOEBE WARD RUSHED around the kitchen, getting ready for the day. As usual, she was swamped with appointments sandwiched between getting her son to and from school. As it was late June, school would be ending soon for the summer and she'd switch to getting him ready for day camp.

"Jamie, get downstairs for breakfast or you'll be late!" she called for him to come join her in the kitchen. By her calculation, they had fifteen minutes for breakfast and then they needed to get into the car for the drive to school.

"I'm here!" He skidded into the room wearing a navy hooded sweatshirt and a pair of black track pants and sneakers, smelling like he'd bathed in Axe. The sharp scent, a combination of citrus and peppermint, was pungent and immediately destroyed her nasal passages and killed her appetite.

She breathed in through her mouth. "What did I

say about overdoing the Axe before school?"

He looked at her with innocent eyes. "I didn't overdo it. You said I had to shower so I did."

And he'd bathed in the body wash and topped it off with matching deodorant. Nice. His teacher was going to have one hell of a migraine if every kid in the room smelled the same way.

"I smell like a man," he said with a cheeky grin.

She bit back a laugh. "You smell like something," she muttered. "Eat your eggs. We need to get moving. I have an early appointment today."

He slid into his chair and began shoveling his food into his mouth. "Are you selling a house?" he asked, glancing at her work suit that she wore for days she was meeting with clients.

"Chew and swallow before talking," she said. "First, I'm meeting a new contractor at Celeste's place," she said of her good friend, Celeste Renault, who'd moved to New York City. "She wants to sell the house and I'm overseeing the renovations. Then I'm showing a listing this afternoon before I pick you up from school."

"Cool." He took two big bites of toast and gulped down his orange juice. "Done." He wiped his mouth on his sleeve and she sighed.

"You're finished. Chickens get done in the oven," she said, correcting his grammar. "Get your backpack together and let's get moving."

He picked up his plate, took it to the sink, rinsed it off, and stuck it in the dishwasher. He was a boy with all the quirky habits that came along with that, but he was a good kid. And considering she'd had him when she'd been sixteen and had been a single parent after that, with only her aunt Joy and her sister Halley for backup, she was damned lucky they'd both turned out okay.

She smiled as he rushed around, repacking the bag that he should have put together the night before. "Slow down and make sure you have everything."

"I do. I'm ready."

She gathered her keys, deciding she'd pick up coffee on her way, and they headed out the door.

She dropped Jamie off at school and waved goodbye, watching until he walked safely inside. Afterwards, she stopped at Grace's Coffee Shop for a large vanilla latte, which she finished on the way over to Celeste's home, a large estate that would sell for a hefty price once renovated. She pulled into the driveway, where a Ford F-150 was already parked. The driver wasn't there, so she exited her vehicle.

If it were later in the day, she'd expect to see more trucks and men working. The dumpster already sat at the head of the driveway, ready for items that were pulled out during construction. Celeste had given both the contractor and Phoebe a set of keys, but Phoebe didn't need to let herself in. The door was open a crack and she toed it the rest of the way, walking in and shutting the door behind her.

She'd never worked with Master's Construction before as they were located outside her hometown of Rosewood Bay, but according to Celeste, they'd won the bidding and came with solid references. Today she was just meeting the contractor in charge for the first time. Her friend wanted an extra set of eyes, as if Celeste were there herself.

"Hello?" Phoebe called out.

"In here!" a masculine voice said, sounding like it came from the far side of the house.

She followed the sound and noticed a man talking on the phone, his back to her. He was tall, well built, muscles defined, as she took him in from behind. And what a behind he had, a tight ass in his faded jeans.

She ogled the sight shamelessly, her gaze traveling up his lean waist and broad shoulders. His dark hair was short and the jet-black color she preferred on a man. He wore a light blue button-down, sleeves rolled up, revealing sexy forearms.

And then he turned to meet her gaze, giving her one raised finger to indicate he needed another minute on the phone. Except she wasn't paying attention to the gesture, because one look at that handsome face, more mature than she remembered but just as good-looking, and she froze.

Vivid blue eyes widened at the sight of her in return.

She wasn't just looking at a stranger, she was staring into the shocked eyes of her son's father, a man she hadn't seen since before she found out she was pregnant.

"Jake?" she whispered, unable to comprehend the fact that she was standing in the same room with her first love. Her first everything.

"Call you back," he said into the phone, disconnecting the call. "Phoebe? Fuck, is that really you?" he asked, sounding as startled as she felt. His voice was the same, yet deeper and infinitely sexier.

"*You're* Master's Construction?" His last name was Nichols. He probably worked for the company, but she was numb at the sight of him, and stupid comments flew from her mouth.

"I'm in charge of the project," he said, gesturing around the house.

"But Master's Construction is located in Thornton," she said of the next town over from Rosewood Bay. "That means you've been nearby all this time?" she asked, still in shock.

"Apparently so," he said, his gaze drinking her in.

"Wow." She'd wanted so badly to find him after

Jamie was born. Her aunt had tried to locate him and failed. Her private investigator had hit a dead end after discovering that Jake had left the group home he'd been sent to, a punishment for being found in bed with Phoebe.

"Let's sit," he suggested. He took her elbow and led her to the nearest sofa, his touch burning through her suit jacket.

She settled in and he joined her, too close and yet too far away.

"Phoebe, God, you look beautiful," he said, his expression warm, his tone a husky sound, reminding her he was more man than boy. He didn't break eye contact, as if afraid if he blinked she'd disappear.

Her cheeks burned at the compliment, and as a pale blonde, when she blushed, the red was noticeable. "Thank you. You look pretty good yourself."

A smile ticked at the corner of his mouth, showing the dimple she remembered.

He was older, his chiseled features more defined, lips full, and she felt like she was looking into the eyes of her son, at what her little boy would look like when he grew up. Panic rose in her throat at the thought.

"What have you been doing with your life?" he asked, leaning in, obviously interested in catching up.

I've been raising your child, she thought, tamping down on near hysteria. She needed to tell him, but she couldn't just blurt out the fact that he had a son. She didn't know anything about his life.

Was he married? Her gaze slid to the finger he'd wear a wedding band on, but there was no sign of a ring. Which didn't mean anything. He might not choose to wear one. Or he could be single but have a girlfriend. Or children of his own.

Her thoughts raced a mile a minute. She definitely wanted time to think things through. To decide how to break it to him and to explain she hadn't shut him out on purpose.

"Phoebe?" he prodded in the wake of her silence.

"I'm a Realtor," she said. "Which is why Celeste trusted me to keep an eye on things while you work."

He nodded in understanding.

"How about you? What have you been up to all this time?" she asked.

"I got into construction after… well, I met a guy who took me under his wing and taught me everything he knows." His big shoulders rolled back and pride sounded in his voice.

"That's good," she murmured, unsure of what to say next.

Silence reigned. Small talk felt awkward considering the weight of the secret lying on her heart. "Umm… listen, I need to go. I forgot some paperwork I have to do for an appointment this afternoon.

Did you need me to show you around the house before I leave?"

His gaze narrowed, showing his confusion at her sudden rush to depart. But he shook his head. "I'm all set. I'm just waiting for the kitchen renovators to show up this morning and the bathroom guys this afternoon."

"Okay, good. Then I'll leave you to it." She rose to her feet, eager for some fresh air. "I'll be back to check in on things in a few days," she said.

She started for the front door, ready to make her escape.

"Phoebe?" he called out, his voice sounding too close.

She turned and looked over her shoulder. He'd risen to his feet and stepped toward her, hand out as if to stop her from leaving. Tall and imposing, he was gorgeous, she thought, feeling like those light blue eyes could see into her soul.

"Yes?" she asked.

He treated her to a warm, engaging smile. "It's good to see you again," he said in a heartfelt voice.

That deep tone rippled through her in a way that was purely sexual. Oh God. So that hadn't changed, either. She was still completely undone by him.

"It's good to see you, too," she whispered back, then turned to go, feeling his eyes on her back as she rushed from the house like the place was on fire.

✧   ✧   ✧

"WHAT THE HELL just happened?" Jake Nichols rubbed a hand along his jaw as he stared at Phoebe's retreating form, her hips swaying in her fitted cream skirt and suit jacket, her silky white-blonde ponytail swaying behind her.

As he'd sat across from her, he'd come to realize she was more mature, still beautiful, but the woman he'd once known intimately was now a stranger. And she'd run from him like he had the plague.

It had been a shock to lay eyes on her. He thought he'd been dreaming. Over the years, in whatever scenarios he'd imagined that involved seeing her again, her being afraid had never been on his radar. But it was clear she hadn't wanted to stick around.

He ran a hand through his hair, his stomach churning and in knots. Phoebe had been it for him. Yeah, they'd been young and pretty damned foolish, but he'd known even then, he'd never find anyone like her again.

And when they'd gotten caught together and he'd taken the fall, the problem child luring the innocent girl into trouble, he'd understood. Hadn't held it against her even though he'd been sent to a group home, the Dawsons the last chance he'd had with a good family. He'd fucked up his opportunity with them, just like he'd done with all the families he'd been sent to before them. The same as he'd done with his single mom, who hadn't been able to handle him. Nobody wanted him after that last screw-up and he'd paid the price.

He'd arrived at the Dawsons' after Phoebe had been there awhile. The family was one of the better ones that had taken him in, but he'd been too much of a shithead to realize it.

Only Phoebe had managed to soothe the anger burning in inside him back then. She'd been the bright light in his time in the system. Smart, studious, and funny, she'd tried to rein him in, but not even for her had he been able to pull back on his difficult tendencies. They'd lie in bed at night, after everyone else in the house had gone to sleep, and talk. She'd weave fantasies about the kind of future they could have together, and damned if he hadn't fallen into believing her.

Losing her had hurt badly. He'd spiraled then, and after the last group home, he'd gotten into even more trouble, but he didn't like to think about that time. Instead he liked to focus on now. And the present was pretty damned good.

He glanced around the massive estate property. When he'd taken on this job, he hadn't known it would bring Phoebe back into his life. But it had.

She might have run out on him, but this time he knew he'd be seeing her again. He'd be able to find out what had happened to her since they'd been separated and hopefully discover more about the woman she'd become.

PHOEBE TORE OUT of Celeste's driveway and headed home, her stomach in knots, panic racing through her. She parked in the circular driveway of the estate where she lived with Jamie in the guesthouse, stopping in front of the main house, where her aunt lived. Her hands still trembled and she needed to calm down before she went inside and gave her aunt the news. That *she* hadn't been able to locate Jake, but he'd walked into Phoebe's life today.

But as much as she'd once wanted to find Jake and tell him about his son, that was how afraid she was of doing it now. Jamie was eleven, almost twelve. So many years had passed. How did she just upend his life that way? How could she not?

She remembered meeting Jake like it was yesterday. Despite her years in foster care, away from her family, Phoebe had maintained her sunny outlook on life thanks to decent families who'd taken her in. She'd taken one look at the bad boy who'd come to the

Dawson house, and she'd fallen for him instantly. She'd believed, as only a young girl could, that she could heal him, and felt horribly guilty after he'd been turned out of their home. It looked as if he'd done all right for himself, though she didn't know the details of the years in between.

A sudden knock on the car window startled her, and Phoebe let out a scream. She glanced up to see her aunt standing by the vehicle, giving her a funny look.

"Are you okay?" Aunt Joy asked.

Phoebe looked into her aunt's green eyes and nodded. Blowing out a breath, she shut off the car and climbed out. "Sorry. I needed a minute before coming inside." She glanced at her aunt, dressed in a pantsuit, her blonde bob sleek and coiffed as usual, her purse in hand.

"Were you coming to see me? I have lunch plans but I'm running early."

Phoebe nodded. "Do you have time to go back inside and talk?"

Her aunt's expression softened. "Of course I do. Let me just call my friend and tell her we need to meet a little later," Aunt Joy said.

That was her aunt, always making time for her. Just like she'd put her life on hold, stepped up, and helped take care of Phoebe's colicky baby. Together they'd gotten through those first long years, and Phoebe had managed to graduate from high school and have her son.

"Are you sure you don't mind?" Phoebe asked, hating to be selfish, but she really did need someone to talk to right now.

"Of course not," her aunt said with a smile.

Phoebe followed Aunt Joy into the huge home where her aunt had grown up.

Aunt Joy stepped away to make her call, leaving Phoebe in the marble entryway. The overly large space, which Aunt Joy told Phoebe had once been cold and forbidding when her aunt's parents were alive, now possessed a warmth thanks to her aunt's personality and décor choices. She'd cozied up the home with oversized furnishings and a distinct lack of fragile items that looked like they would break if you merely glanced at them the wrong way.

Instead there were family photos of Phoebe and Halley as teenagers and Jamie in various phases of childhood. Her son had grown up toddling down these long hallways, and not once had she worried about him touching the wrong things.

"Okay, I'm all yours. My friend asked if we could reschedule lunch anyway. She has a cold and isn't feeling well. So I have all the time you need."

"Great. Can we sit?" Phoebe asked.

Her aunt nodded. They headed to the large kitchen

that, again, her aunt had changed from a room meant only for cooking by staff to a warm place where a family could congregate.

Phoebe placed her purse on the table and sat down before turning to her aunt. "You're not going to believe what happened today."

"I'm listening."

Phoebe swallowed hard. "Remember how you hired an investigator to try and find Jake? Jamie's father?"

"Yes…" her aunt said somewhat warily.

"Well, I walked into Celeste's house today to meet the contractor and there he was. Standing there. Right in front of me." She still couldn't believe she'd run into him like that. Out of the blue. "I mean, what are the odds?"

Her aunt paled. "Oh my God."

"I know. He's been living in Thornton all this time," she said.

Her aunt curled her hands together, looking as shaken as Phoebe felt. "What happened? What did you two say to each other?"

Phoebe was mortified at the answer. "I ran away," she whispered. "He looks so much like Jamie it completely blew my mind. And he asked me what I'd been up to and I thought, *I've been raising your son.* So I panicked and took off."

"Oh, honey." Aunt Joy reached out a comforting hand, patting her on the arm.

"I'm going to have to tell him about Jamie. I just needed time to figure out how to do it. What to say to him." She twisted her hands together, the nerves still jumbled in her stomach.

Aunt Joy leaned forward and sighed. "Phoebe, do you remember how young you were when you came to live with me? You were practically a baby having a baby."

"I remember." Her aunt had just pulled her from foster care after finding out about Phoebe and her sister from their drug-addict mother, who, prior to that, Joy hadn't seen or heard from in years. Then Phoebe had discovered she was pregnant. She counted herself lucky that her aunt hadn't forced her to give the baby up for adoption... or worse.

Instead her aunt had enabled her to remain in school and keep the baby, something Phoebe had wanted with a desperation. It didn't take a psychologist to figure out that a kid who grew up in the system, even in a good home where the people welcomed her, would still be searching for love and acceptance of her own. She'd lost Jake but she'd had the chance to have and keep his baby. Her baby, who would love her unconditionally.

She'd always owe Aunt Joy for that and she

grasped her aunt's hand. "You were there for me every step of the way. You were my rock and I'll always be grateful."

"So you know I only wanted the very best for you and for Jamie, right?"

Phoebe nodded. "Of course I know that. What's going on?"

Her aunt blinked, tears forming in her eyes.

"What is it?" Phoebe asked, more forcefully this time.

"When I told you that the investigator couldn't find Jake, that wasn't the truth."

"What?" she asked, her voice rising. She couldn't believe her ears. She had to have heard wrong. Her aunt wouldn't lie to her about that.

"My private investigator *did* find Jake, but I had very good reasons for not telling you."

She couldn't imagine even one. "Go on," she said through clenched teeth, trying to hold herself together. Reminding herself this was the woman who'd given her everything.

Aunt Joy let out a sigh. "We started looking for Jake right after you gave birth to Jamie, remember?"

Phoebe nodded. The first months after coming to live with her aunt had been filled with fear and learning whether or not she could trust this new relative who'd suddenly appeared. On the heels of the change in environment, of being reunited with her sister, Phoebe had discovered she was pregnant. Between starting a new school, dealing with her reality, and knowing she was going to keep the baby, she'd been totally overwhelmed. It hadn't been until after she'd had Jamie that she'd been focused enough to think about looking for Jake.

"When I did find him," her aunt went on, "he wasn't in a place that was right for you or your baby."

Phoebe narrowed her gaze. "What does that mean? And why did you think it was your call to make?"

"Because he was in prison!"

Phoebe sucked in a startled breath. "He was where?"

"In prison. And you'd just had a baby. I didn't think bringing a convicted felon into your life was the right thing to do."

"Oh my God." She braced her head in her hands and tried to process her aunt's words and motives. She understood… and she didn't. "What was he incarcerated for?" she asked in a trembling voice.

"The answer to that question also played into my decision," her aunt said, her sadness and regret clear. "Assault and battery."

"Jesus." She tried to put herself back all those years, to remember the angry teenager Jake had been.

Although sweet with her, with people he distrusted

he'd been quick to blow up. He'd possessed a bad temper and had fought with the boys in his prior foster home, and he often gave the Dawsons' biological son, Eric, a hard time, but he'd never gotten physical with him.

And Phoebe had always been able to calm him with a soothing word or touch. So for him to have beat someone up badly enough to end up in jail? She didn't want to believe it, but on this, her aunt wouldn't lie.

She rubbed her palms against her aching temples, confused and hurting.

"I didn't want someone dangerous near you or Jamie. I made a judgment call and I can't apologize for wanting you safe."

Phoebe shook her head. "I just wish you'd let me decide that for myself."

"You were young and would have been blinded by love. I did what I had to do," her aunt said, standing by her decision.

Phoebe swallowed hard and pushed herself to her feet. "I need to think. About everything."

"Are you going to tell him about Jamie? What if he's still dangerous?"

"What if he's not?" Phoebe said, automatically defending Jake. That had always been second nature to her, and apparently not seeing him in over a decade hadn't changed that instinct.

She breathed into her hands. "I have to spend time with him while he's working on Celeste's. I'll see what he's like now and then I'll decide what to do." Except in her heart, she couldn't help but think he deserved to know about his child.

He'd missed so much time already. Was it really right of her to withhold more? Even though he'd been in jail for a violent crime, maybe there was an explanation that made sense.

Besides, people changed and grew up. He had an important job, was trusted by his boss to run this huge estate project. All that spoke to his character.

"I really do need to go." She rose to her feet.

"Don't leave angry," her aunt pleaded.

"I'm not angry. I'm sad. And I just need time to get over everything, that's all." Time to process before she had to put on a cheerful façade and face her little boy after school.

Jamie knew as much of the truth as he was capable of understanding, that Phoebe had loved his daddy but they'd been separated before he was born and she hadn't been able to find him in the time since.

It pained her that Jamie didn't have a father, especially because up until Halley met Kane, Jamie hadn't had a male influence in his life. He'd been surrounded by loving, caring women. Kane, in the time he'd been with Halley, almost a year now, had come by to take Jamie on boys' outings. They played basketball and Kane played catch with him, but the fact was, Jamie didn't have a dad.

Except he did.

Jake was back and Phoebe had to decide what to do about that.

Chapter Two

A FTER A LONG week at work, Jake pulled into the parking lot of Master's Construction and cut the engine. As he climbed out of the truck, he thought about how important the Renault estate job was to him. It was the biggest opportunity Brent Master, his boss and mentor, along with his ex-father-in-law, had given him to date. The chance to oversee a project of this magnitude on his own, from start to finish—from initial assessment to successful bid, hiring subcontractors, and bringing the project in successfully, within budget and on time—was a big deal.

And he knew, because Brent was clear on the subject and because despite the divorce, he thought of Jake like a son, Jake had a real chance to buy the company from him when Brent was ready to retire. Jake just needed to prove himself as capable of running a business as he was of the more hands-on aspects of the job. Not that he could see Brent retiring anytime soon, and Jake wasn't ready to see the man leave the company he'd built and loved.

He pushed open the door and let himself into the building where the company was located. More like a house from the outside, Master's took up the bottom level and other businesses leased space inside, including an architectural firm on the top floor.

"Hi," Brent said, greeting him as he walked through the doorway.

Wearing his standard khaki pants and a pale green button-down shirt, his salt-and-pepper hair graying more by the day, he otherwise hadn't changed since Jake met him all those years ago.

"Hi, yourself. What are you still doing here?" Jake asked, although he knew the answer. As owner of the company, Brent liked to stick around until the very end of the day. Jake wished he'd cut back and relax a little, but it wasn't in the man's nature.

"How's the job going? Anything you want to go over before I leave?"

Jake shook his head. "It's going smoothly, at least in the early stages. But of course, that means I should be wary," he said wryly. Brent had taught him never to take anything for granted and to watch out for all aspects of the job.

With a chuckle, Brent patted Jake on the shoulder. "You remembered," he said proudly.

Jake smiled. "Of course. I learned from the best."

Brent walked over to his desk and grabbed his keys.

"Are you going to get dinner before you head home?" Jake asked, wanting to make sure the man had a decent meal.

As a bachelor, Jake cooked for himself, but he pretty much sucked at it. Takeout was a staple for him, as it was for Brent since he had lost his wife a few years ago.

"I actually have leftovers in the fridge. And I'd invite you over but I only have enough for one," he said, laughing.

"I hear you. Just making sure you don't starve."

Jake liked to look out for Brent as much as he'd once looked out for Jake. After he'd done his time in prison, his parole officer had introduced Jake to Brent, a man who took in troubled kids, taught them a trade, and gave them a sense of purpose. There'd been kids before Jake, but he'd stuck around long after he could have branched out on his own.

Brent had brought Jake into his family and his business. He'd taught him about craft and pride in your work, educating him in every aspect of construction. There was no job too small for Jake to learn, and he'd done it, at first to please Brent, the man who'd given him a chance, and later because he'd begun to believe in himself.

"I hear you have plans to go to the circus with Lindsay and Callie," Jake said of his ex-wife and almost six-year-old daughter. "Callie can't wait to go."

Brent grinned. "I can't wait to take her. I wish…" He trailed off and Jake knew what the older man meant.

"I know. But it's better Lindsay and I do things with Callie separately. Anything else sends the wrong message to them both." The last thing Jake wanted to do was confuse his little girl or make his ex think he desired to get back together.

"I understand. Okay then, have a good weekend," Brent said, waving a hand as he walked out the door.

"You, too." Settling at his desk, Jake shuffled some papers and made a list of calls he needed to get to on Monday morning before heading over to the Renault place.

And maybe see Phoebe. She'd been on his mind a lot since their initial encounter, but she hadn't shown up at the house again.

Once the shock of seeing her had worn off, questions flooded his mind. Was she married or otherwise attached? His entire body stiffened, automatically rejecting the notion. Or was she single and available? Would she relax enough around him for her green eyes to warm up, and would she really let them catch up and talk? Or would she continue to keep him at arm's length? All questions only she could answer, and he looked forward to finding out.

PHOEBE AND JAMIE spent the rainy weekend at home. He'd finished his homework and spent his free time playing X-Box, games and Legos. She cooked dinners and tried to relax and enjoy the quiet time without obsessing about how Jake might react when she told him the truth. She wouldn't even let her mind go to having to tell Jamie she'd found his father. One baby step at a time, she told herself. That's how she'd handle things.

Phoebe arrived at Celeste's on Monday morning, if not prepared, at least forewarned that she'd be seeing Jake again.

As she entered, she heard and saw men at work, both on the kitchen, tearing out the existing cabinets, and as she meandered farther through the house, in the master bath, also gutting the fixtures that were there. As far as she could tell, everything was proceeding according to schedule.

Gathering her courage, she went in search of Jake. She found him outside the kitchen, standing on the patio with another man, and from the tense posture of both, and the frustrated expression on their faces, it looked like they were arguing.

She didn't want to get in the way, so she stood in the doorway and waited for them to finish their discussion.

"I need reliable people," Jake was saying, his voice tight. "Not someone who's going to roll out of bed hungover and show up an hour late." To emphasize his point, Jake pointed at the face of his watch.

"Come on, man. Cut me some slack. I had an argument with my wife and couldn't even sleep at home last night."

Phoebe took a good look at the other man and realized his eyes were bloodshot, his clothing wrinkled.

"No slack, JD. Not this time. You're hungover, which means you aren't safe around the equipment. You're fired," Jake said in a firm voice.

"But—"

Jake shook his head. "Three strikes," he reminded the man with a shake of his head.

"Hard-ass," the guy muttered and stormed past Jake, deliberately bumping his shoulder against Jake's as he passed.

Phoebe held her breath, wondering if Jake would take the provocation to go after the other man. Instead he checked something on his clipboard and, with a groan, started for the door leading to the house.

He glanced up and realized she was waiting there.

"Phoebe," he said, a slow, welcoming smile curving his lips.

Not the actions of a short-tempered man, easy to rile up, she thought, relaxing her shoulders. "Good morning," she said with a wave. "I didn't want to interrupt."

"JD's a good guy but his work ethic leaves a lot to be desired." Jake gestured for her to turn and walk back into the kitchen with him, which she did. "Unfortunately, JD let his personal life intrude on the job one too many times."

"Then you did what you had to do," she said, impressed with the matter-of-fact way he'd handled himself with the other man.

Jake placed the clipboard on the counter and faced her. "So I was thinking about you over the weekend."

"You were?" Because heaven knew she'd thought about him.

His blue eyes bored into hers. "Many times," he said in a gruff voice. "And I was hoping we could get together and catch up."

She swallowed hard. She hadn't thought he'd ask to go out, but now that she thought about it, sitting down with him and talking about the past would give her insight into the kind of man he had become. It would enable her to become more comfortable with the idea of telling him about his son.

"I'd like that," she said, smiling at the thought. "I'm curious about what you've been up to all these years."

He blinked, obviously startled she'd agreed so easily. "Okay then. Does Saturday night work?"

"I have to get a—" She bit her tongue before the word *babysitter* could fall out. "New outfit," she said inanely, folding her arms across her chest.

His gaze drifted, following the movement. She glanced down, realizing the gesture had the unintended consequence of pulling her top down lower on her chest. With the top two buttons already undone, her cleavage peeked out from the parted blouse, swells of flesh and hints of her peach lace bra showing through the vee.

Blushing, she dropped her arms and fluffed her shirt in an attempt to pull herself together.

A knowing flush highlighted his cheekbones. "So where do you want to go?" he asked, keeping them on the subject of dinner. "I was going to ask you what your favorite restaurant is."

"I love the Blue Wall in town. They have the best desserts."

He nodded. "The Blue Wall it is. I'll pick you up at seven if you give me directions to your place."

And have Jake run into Jamie or see evidence of her son around the house if he happened to end up inside? "Thanks but I don't mind meeting you there."

"Okay, then—" Whatever he was going to say next was cut off by the sharp ring of his cell phone.

"Excuse me." He pulled his phone from his back jeans pocket, glanced at the screen, and frowned before accepting the call. "Hello?"

He listened, then said, "I'm at work but if it's an emergency…" He paused again while the person on the other end obviously spoke. "Fine. Sure, I'll stop at the drugstore on the way over. Gatorade, too?" Some more listening. Then, "And ginger ale. Got it." He sighed. "See you soon," he said and disconnected the call.

Jake met Phoebe's gaze briefly before glancing away. "That was my ex-wife."

The words hit her harder than they should have. "I see."

Awkwardness stretched between them and then he spoke again. "My daughter has a stomach virus, and she asked me to pick up a few things."

And that hurt, too. It shouldn't. They'd been little more than children when they were together last, but still, his life had gone on, in a very different way than hers. She'd had her baby but hadn't otherwise moved on. Not for lack of trying to find a good man. No one had sparked her interest enough to even bring him around her child. Meanwhile, he'd found someone to love, had a child… which meant her son had a half sibling. Oh my God.

"Phoebe?" Serious eyes locked on hers and a wealth of emotion passed between them.

"How old is your daughter?" she managed to ask as if nothing were wrong.

He grinned at the question. "Callie is six." He scrolled through his phone and held out a photograph. "Here." He showed her a photograph of a little girl with long, dark curls and semi-grown-in front teeth.

"She's adorable," Phoebe murmured. She could see hints of Jake in her expression and her dark hair.

"Thanks. I think so but I'm biased." He laughed. "I need to go pick up what Lindsay needs. That's my ex."

She nodded in understanding.

"If you don't come by again during the week, I'll see you Saturday night at 7:15? At the Blue Wall?"

She drew a deep breath and nodded. The work on the house was going to take the better part of two months, if not longer. She didn't need to come by every day. She'd be here more often as installation on various rooms began.

"I'll see you Saturday," she agreed, knowing now they'd have much more to talk about than she'd ever realized.

✧   ✧   ✧

JAKE RUSHED THROUGH the grocery store, collecting the items Lindsay had asked him for. The checkout line was long, which drove him crazy as he waited to be taken. Finally, he put the bags in the back seat of his truck and headed over to his ex-wife's house, the house he used to live in with her.

On the drive over, he couldn't help but wish he'd had the time to tell Phoebe about his marriage and daughter in a different way. Less rushed. More caring about her feelings. He'd caught the surprise on her face at the word *ex-wife* and the follow up comment about his daughter. Not that either of them owed the other anything, but still, he could see it had been a shock and not necessarily a good one.

With a groan, he pulled into the driveway and parked, letting himself out of the car. He gathered the packages and headed to the front door. He rang the bell and he heard footsteps soon after.

His ex pulled the door open and greeted him with a smile. She wore a pair of jeans and a long-sleeve flowing shirt, her long brown hair falling over her shoulder, makeup done up, too. Lindsay was an attractive woman, and that hadn't changed since the divorce. Whenever he saw her, she was well put together. She certainly didn't look like she'd been dealing with a kid with a stomach virus.

"You came," she said, sounding relieved.

He stepped inside. "Of course I did. How's the princess?"

She took the packages from him and he followed her into the kitchen. Before she could answer, his daughter came bounding toward him.

"Daddy!" She jumped up so he could catch her in his arms the way he usually did, and as always happened, his heart clenched inside his chest. He adored this kid. "Whoa, baby. Don't you have a stomach bug?"

She met his gaze with her big-eyed brown one. "I had a bellyache this morning and we were out of ginger ale."

He frowned at his ex, who ignored him.

"I feel better now, though, and I want to play with Ally," she said of her best friend. "Can I? Please?" she asked without missing a beat.

"What happened to her stomach virus?" he asked, because those were the words Lindsay had used on the phone, and in his book, that usually meant a mess on one or both ends and a very sick child.

Lindsay leaned against the Formica kitchen counter. "No playing with Ally today. You didn't feel well enough to go to school, so no playdate for you."

"Pooh," Callie said.

"Pooh?" he asked, laughing.

"It's a new expression she picked up. Give Daddy

a kiss and then go rest," Lindsay said to Callie.

"Okay, Mommy." He bent down and she grasped his cheeks, putting a smacking kiss against his skin. "Bye, Daddy."

"Bye, baby. I'll call you later."

She skipped out of the room, no sign of illness, especially not a stomach virus.

"What's going on?" he asked.

He met Lindsay's sheepish gaze and she visibly swallowed hard. "Callie told you herself she had a stomachache."

He held back a few choice phrases and instead focused on the issue at hand. "Hardly the virus you insinuated. Do you really think it's fair to ask me to leave work because you're out of ginger ale?" he asked, not bothering to hide the annoyance in his tone.

It had been this way since the divorce, never mind that Lindsay had instigated the separation and ultimate result. She would constantly find reasons to demand his time and attention, and though he would do anything for his daughter, sometimes Lindsay took advantage of that fact and pushed him too far.

"How did I know that she wouldn't get sick in the car on the way to the grocery store?" Lindsay turned her back and began to unpack the bag she'd put on the counter earlier.

His ex had wanted the divorce up until she'd asked

for it. Jake had the feeling she'd wanted him to fight it, to fight for her, but he'd known she wasn't happy. Hell, neither was he. He'd just never wanted to take that step if he could make his marriage work, but when she'd asked, he'd accepted that it was over.

He'd loved her, but he realized he hadn't been in love with her. As a result, he hadn't been giving her the kind of attention she deserved, and he'd opted not to prolong the inevitable. But she'd never really let go, and that was becoming more apparent and more of an issue.

He waited until she'd put the soda in the refrigerator and turned back to face him. "Lindsay, you can only call me for real emergencies." *We're not married anymore*, he thought, but bit back the words, not wanting to hurt her feelings by shoving the obvious in her face.

"She's your daughter, too," she reminded him, sounding petulant and upset.

"And I'm there for her on my weekends and anytime she really needs me. I'm sure you have friends who could have stopped by the supermarket for you without calling me to drop everything. I'm busy," he told her, in case she really needed to hear it again. "Now if you'll excuse me, I'm going to get back to work."

She stood by the corner of the counter and looked

at him through sad eyes. "Whatever you say, Jake."

He forced himself to ignore her pitiful look, reminding himself she was still trying to get him back, after all these years. They'd been divorced for the last four, so she ought to know the drill by now.

He paid alimony and child support. He had partial custody and loved spending time with his daughter. But he and Lindsay weren't a family. And never would be again.

SATURDAY ARRIVED QUICKLY, too quickly, and ironically, Phoebe really didn't know what to wear. Her work suits were her uniform she wore during the day and didn't fit for a Saturday night dinner. Not that she'd call it a date, but she wanted to feel more feminine than business professional. Her jeans were too casual, and she didn't have something in between.

Which explained why her sister had arrived with an armful of dresses for Phoebe to try on.

Halley laid the dresses across Phoebe's bed. "I didn't bring you any of my flowy Bohemian dresses because that's not your type, but I did have a few more structured dresses for you to choose from. This one I wore when I went to meet with the owner of an art gallery in Manhattan," she said.

Her sister had gone from almost hermit to someone not afraid to put herself and her paintings out for the world to see. It thrilled Phoebe to no end that Halley had finally put the past behind her and moved on with her future. And Kane Harmon.

Phoebe took in the cream-colored sleeveless dress and smiled. "It's my color." Phoebe preferred neutrals in her clothing choice. The dress also didn't look too fitted, which would work because Phoebe's chest was larger than her sister's.

She peeled off her jeans and tee shirt, knowing her son was at a sleepover with a friend, so she didn't have to worry about him barging in. She shimmied the dress over her head and adjusted it around her hips.

"Let's see," Halley said.

Phoebe turned toward her sister and smoothed her hands over the material. "Well?"

Halley grinned, clapping her hands in approval. "I knew that would be the one. You don't even need to try on the others."

"That's a huge load off my mind," she murmured.

"This is what we missed out on," Halley said sadly. "Helping each other get dressed for dates, hanging out as teenagers, confiding in each other."

They didn't look alike, Halley with her light brown hair and Phoebe with her pale blonde, Phoebe with green eyes, Halley with light blue.

"But we have now and that makes us lucky,"

Phoebe said, taking the more optimistic view as she always tried to do.

Still, she couldn't help but marvel, as she often did, that they'd been reunited again after ten years in different foster homes. As angry as she was at her aunt for keeping Jake's whereabouts from her, she knew she wouldn't hold a grudge. Not against the woman who had brought Phoebe and Halley back together.

It was after their mother had been arrested for drug possession and intent to sell that Aunt Joy found out about Phoebe and Halley. Their mother, Meg, apparently had called her much younger sister and informed Joy that she had had children, two in foster care.

According to Aunt Joy, their youngest sister, Juliette, had gone to live with her father just before Meg lost custody of her older girls due to neglect. Sober and a bit remorseful, at least at the time, Meg had admitted she'd all but handed Juliette to her biological father in exchange for a substantial amount of cash and signed over custody. Meg had never revealed Juliette's father's last name and they'd never found their sister.

"You're thinking about her, aren't you?" Halley asked, interrupting Phoebe's thoughts and rightly reading her mind.

She had been thinking of her mother. "I hate her,

but it always comes back to her choices and her behavior," Phoebe muttered. "I try not to dwell on her but sometimes it happens."

"I know. Me, too," Halley admitted.

And since her mother was a compulsive drug addict, liar, and recently a thief, stealing from Halley, they'd had firsthand knowledge of the fact that their mother hadn't, and would never, change.

Halley sat down on the bed, curling a leg beneath her, a serious expression on her face. "Let's focus on you, shall we? Are you planning to tell Jake about Jamie tonight?"

Phoebe drew a deep breath. "I'm not *planning* ahead. I want to see how the conversation goes. I need to see if he tells me about having been in prison." She'd told Halley about what their aunt had done during a phone call they'd shared soon after Phoebe found out the truth.

"And if he doesn't?"

"Then I have to ask him about it. I need to understand what happened before I bring him around my son." She ran her hands up and down her bare arms, where goose bumps had risen.

"Is there a reason you could accept and still let him around Jamie?"

Phoebe swallowed hard. She'd done nothing but think about this since she'd found out. "I'd like to think so. I want to believe my gut feeling about him is the right one, that he's a good man who somehow ended up in a bad situation."

Her sister nodded. "I saw a lot of angry kids in foster care who acted out," Halley said quietly. "I'd also like to believe the ones I think were good deep down would have straightened out as they got older."

Unlike their mother, the poster child for not being able to overcome the past. But she wasn't going there again in her mind.

Instead she walked over to her closet and riffled through until she found the black Pashmina shawl she wanted to throw over her shoulders in case it was cool in the restaurant.

Then she stepped into a pair of cream pumps that matched the dress. Hair and makeup were already complete, so she was good to go and she let out a shaky breath.

Halley walked up to her and grasped her hands. "Don't be nervous. You can do this."

"He's divorced and he has a daughter," she whispered to her sister.

Halley shot her a knowing look. "Life went on. That's normal, right?"

Phoebe nodded. "It's just… I know we were kids and we never expected to see each other again. I just didn't anticipate the knowledge hurting and it did."

She swallowed over the lump in her throat, knowing she had to get over it if she was going to deal with Jake in a rational way tonight.

"I understand. I wish there was something I could do to make tonight easier."

"Talking to you helped ease the anxiety and butterflies in my stomach. I can handle this."

Halley smiled. "Yes, you can."

She'd use the strength she had to face Jake and whatever the future held. Whether or not tonight was the night she told him he had a son remained to be seen.

Chapter Three

J AKE HAD NEVER been to the Blue Wall. The same
could be said of most places in the town of Rosewood Bay. True, he didn't live far from here, but he'd
always gravitated to the other side of his town of
Thornton and the neighboring areas. Rosewood Bay
was all new to him.

The Blue Wall was a nice restaurant, cobblestone
outside. One side of the building housed a bar with
live music on the weekends, and the other was an
upscale restaurant. As he waited for Phoebe in the
hostess area, he took in the aqua-blue walls and
enormous wall-size fish tank in the main dining area
with interest. The décor lived up to the restaurant's
name.

"You could have been seated," Phoebe said, coming up behind him.

He turned to face her, blown away by her beauty.
"I wanted to wait," he said, his gaze taking her in. The

last two times he'd seen her, she'd been wearing a businesslike suit, her hair pulled back, either in a bun or a ponytail.

Tonight she was wearing a cream-colored sleeveless dress. She'd removed her shawl already and it was hanging over one arm. Her hair fell around her shoulders, light blonde framing her delicate features. And the dress itself was fitted around her full breasts, which were larger now than he remembered. His fingers itched to touch her, so he curled them into tight fists.

The hostess walked them to their table. Along the way, Phoebe stopped a few times for hellos, introducing him to people she worked with, was friendly with, or had sold a home to.

"I'm so sorry," she said when they finally made it to their table. "I wish I could have walked by all those people, but it would have been rude."

He grinned. "You haven't changed." He'd always enjoyed her outgoing personality and wouldn't alter her nature a bit.

She laughed. "I guess not. I'm still a people person."

Instead of a table, the hostess took them to a circular booth, and they ended up sitting side by side. Though he wouldn't have minded staring at her from across the table, he enjoyed being this close to her, too. Her fragrant scent aroused him, making him grateful for the darkened ambience and the cover of the table over his growing erection.

"Your waiter will be with you shortly," the hostess said, leaving them with their menus as she walked away.

"Everything here is good." With a gentle nudge, Phoebe slid his menu toward him. "You can't go wrong with anything you order."

He opened the menu for a quick glance, choosing his meal and shutting it again. He wasn't fussy about his food and he'd rather be talking to her.

"So." He pushed the leather-bound book aside. "How have you been, really?"

"Good." She smiled as she answered, evidencing the truth of her statement. "Life since I saw you last has been full of surprises, actually."

He leaned closer. "Tell me everything."

That pretty grin faltered but she obviously caught herself and managed another less-genuine smile. He wondered what was behind the sudden shift, but he didn't have time to ponder for long, because she jumped right in to elaborate.

"Let's see. I'd have to go back to the beginning. Shortly after we… after you left the Dawsons', an aunt came and claimed me. Aunt Joy took me out of foster care along with my sister Halley, who'd been in another foster home. Do you remember me mentioning her?"

"How could I forget?" One of the things that had pained her was losing touch with her sister. She'd often talked about how much she wished she could find her. "That's amazing," he said of her aunt.

She nodded. "After ten years of being alone, I suddenly had a family again." This time the smile reached her eyes.

He was happy for her because he knew that, despite her always cheery outlook, she'd been lonely inside, searching for love. And for the time they were together, he'd tried to give it to her.

Despite his inability to deal with most people, they'd bonded intimately. He'd wanted to be everything to her back then... because she'd been everything to him.

"It really was like a miracle."

He shifted so he could look at her as they spoke, and his thigh brushed against hers. His skin burned where they'd accidentally touched, the heat going straight to his cock. Jesus. She still had a huge effect on him.

"Do you know why your aunt didn't come get you before?" he managed to ask, glad his voice didn't betray the desire coursing through his veins.

She nodded. "I do."

"Hi, folks. Can I get you something to drink?" the

waitress asked, interrupting the flow of conversation.

Phoebe ordered a glass of Chardonnay and he chose a beer on tap.

She waited until they were alone again before continuing. "My aunt told us a lot about my mother that I didn't know." She glanced down at her hands, which she'd laced together on top of the table. "My family is pretty dysfunctional," she murmured. "It seems that after my mother married my father, my grandparents disowned her because he'd enlisted in the army and had no prospects for a future that they approved of."

"That's pretty damned judgmental," he couldn't help but say.

"You're telling me." A sad expression crossed her face. "A few years later, Dad was killed in action and Mom fell apart. She was holding down a job but she got hurt, began using painkillers, and became addicted. She began spending the nights in bars, and our little sister, Juliette, was born shortly after."

She drew a deep breath and continued. "Instead of stepping up then, my mother's parents, wonderful humans that they were, refused to help Mom out. Aunt Joy was eight years younger than mom, and her parents never even told her that her sister had had kids." She shook her head, obviously still stunned by the story after all these years.

He couldn't fathom what kind of parents turned

their back on their own child. There was nothing Callie could do that would make him walk away from her. "So how did your aunt find out about you and your sister?"

She took a sip of water and met his gaze. "Mom was arrested for possession and intent to sell. She sobered up and called her sister to tell her that Halley and I were in the system." She shrugged, as if it were that simple.

He placed a hand over hers, curling his fingers around her smaller one. "God. I'm sorry, Phoebe. For all of it."

A long, lingering look passed between them, one that began as a sympathetic one and quickly morphed to a more heated sense of awareness.

"And here are your drinks." The waitress returned, placing a glass of white wine in front of Phoebe and the beer before Jake, interrupting the heated, albeit quiet, moment.

"Can I take your orders?" the woman asked, pen and paper in hand.

Phoebe shook her head as if to clear it. "I'll have the salmon and rice pilaf," she said. "And what kind of vegetable do you have tonight?"

"Spinach? Broccoli?"

"Spinach," she said, handing over the menu.

The waitress turned her gaze to his. "Sir?"

"The pork chop," he said. "Baked potato and spinach." He glanced at Phoebe and she laughed.

"The spinach is delicious," Phoebe said.

He grinned.

"Thank you," the waitress said, turning and walking away.

Phoebe met his gaze, the heated awareness gone. He hoped it wasn't for good. The fact that there was still such a strong sense of awareness between them told him things were far from over. Nor did he want their relationship to be in the past.

"So let's talk about you," she said.

He shook his head. "Not so fast. Your story was just getting interesting. "How is Halley? Are you two close?" he asked, curious to know everything about her life.

She nodded, her eyes lighting up. "She's incredible. You'd really like her."

"I hope I get the chance to meet her, then. And you mentioned another sister?"

"Juliette." True sadness crossed Phoebe's face. "Mom gave her to her father in exchange for a lump sum payment and relinquishing custody." Her lips twisted in disgust. "To this day, she hasn't told anyone Juliette's father's last name or where he's located," she said wistfully.

Her mother had sold her own child. Son of a bitch.

"You wish you could locate her, don't you?"

She nodded. "Mom resurfaced about a year ago. Halley tried to trust her and got burned badly. She never had the chance to ask her about Juliette, not that Mom offered up the information, either." She shook her head. "But... the good news is that Aunt Joy turned out to be great and I got Halley back, too."

"And your grandparents?" he asked of the people who hadn't deserved to have children.

"They passed away before my return."

And good riddance, he thought.

"Now it's your turn." She lifted her glass and took a sip of wine, her small pink tongue coming out to smooth over her lips.

He wanted a taste of that tongue, he thought, then shifted in his seat, his thigh once again coming into contact with hers.

She let out a small exhale, one he noticed because he was hyperaware of her at the moment. Both her inadvertent touch and her reaction didn't help his own state of arousal.

Ignoring his body's response to being near her, he cleared his throat. "Me. What do you want to know?" To start at the beginning meant that he'd have to reveal the truth about what had happened to him in the intervening years.

He wasn't as much embarrassed about his past as

he regretted the choices he'd made and wished for a do-over in some ways. But then, who didn't have things they preferred hadn't happened? Some more than most?

"Are you sure you want to know?" he asked.

Her pretty green eyes grew intense. "I wouldn't have asked if I didn't."

He drew in a deep breath. "I spent time in prison," he admitted, getting the truth out without beating around the bush.

She slowly lowered her glass to the table. "I know."

Her words couldn't have shocked him more. "You do?"

She nodded, biting down on her lower lip. "A little while after my aunt *rescued* me," she said with air quotes around the word, "I wanted to find you. She told me she had no luck after the group home, but when I told her I ran into you the other day? She confessed that she'd lied. She discovered you were incarcerated and opted not to tell me." She shook her head, tears in her eyes. "I just need to know why. Why would you end up in jail?"

He shook his head. "Stupidity?"

She waited patiently, so he went on, describing what had happened during one of his hotheaded moments. "I was at a bar with a few friends. A big guy hit on a woman who had told him to go away. He wouldn't take no for an answer. I got in the middle, swung, the guy went down and hit his head. Knocked him out. He ended up in the hospital, needing surgery from the blow to the head. I was arrested for assault and battery. Given my record, no one really gave a shit that I was looking out for someone, you know?"

She reached out and took his hand, wrapping her fingers around his, offering comfort. "That's awful."

He rolled his shoulders in a lighthearted shrug he didn't necessarily feel about the subject. Prison had been brutal. He'd had to watch his back and make sure he played it smart with the other inmates. Six months had never felt so long.

Then again, he knew things had happened for a reason. "I had a temper back then. We both know it." Looking back, he could see his path to prison had been clear and all his own damned fault.

After his father had left, never to be heard from again, Jake had begun acting out. As a teenager, he'd graduated from mouthing off to his mom to cutting school, missing curfew, and ultimately getting in with the wrong crowd. He'd moved on to petty theft, minor drugs and lots of alcohol, and being dragged home by the police.

After one too many run-ins with the cops and the justice system, he'd managed to get himself pulled from his mother's house and tossed into foster care. His mom had been beside herself, and he'd spent many of his adult years making his behavior up to her. So winding up behind bars hadn't come as a surprise.

He was just damned grateful he'd ended up where he was today. "Six months inside taught me the importance of mellowing out when I was released. I learned to take a step back before jumping into the fray or acting on my angry impulses."

Her eyes were still damp as she looked at him. He didn't want her feeling sorry for him, and when she sniffed, one lone tear dripped down her cheek.

He reached out and swiped at it with his thumb. "Don't cry for me," he told her in a gruff voice.

"I'm just sorry. You didn't deserve what happened. Not when you got thrown out of the Dawsons' and it doesn't sound like you deserved prison, either," she said, her expression somber.

"I've dealt with it. Besides, it led me to a good place."

She seemed to perk up at the proclamation. "How so?"

Just then, the waitress arrived and served their meal. While they ate, he told her about how he'd met Brent. "My parole officer liked me, go figure. So he introduced me to Brent Master, a man who took in kids like me, taught them a trade in construction."

"That's wonderful," she exclaimed.

He nodded. "We just clicked. He was like the father I never had…" He drew a breath and forced out the next words because they had to be said. "And I married his daughter."

Silence followed that declaration.

Using her fork, she toyed with her rice before meeting his gaze. "I'd hoped you'd find happiness," she said at last. "But I admit, for the girl I used to be, it hurts to think of you with someone else."

"What about for the woman you are now? Does she hurt to think of me with someone else?" he asked, deciding to push her a little. Because during the time he'd sat here listening to her, he'd been drawn back into her orbit.

There was something compelling about Phoebe, at least for him—her eternal optimism, genuine love of life and people, and her big heart, all of which had remained and grown since he'd seen her last. She'd fulfilled the promise of youth, and as a woman, she was special.

Her startled gaze met his at the pointed question. She bit down on her lower lip as she thought about how to answer him.

"Of course it hurts me to think about you with someone else," she murmured at last. "You used to belong to me."

He wondered if he could belong to her again or if too much time had passed. "It would hurt me to think of you with another guy. Has there been anyone serious? Is there?" he asked.

Her gaze hot on his, she shook her head. "No. There've been men... but no one who meant enough to me to..." She trailed off, wrinkling her nose in thought before continuing. "No one got past my walls. And despite how open I seem to be, trust me, I have them."

He expelled a long breath he hadn't been aware of holding, relieved he didn't have to deal with the emotion of jealousy, sad that she had to cope with it on her end. But he couldn't regret his time with Lindsay, not when it had given him Callie. Not something he intended to say aloud now.

Instead he reached out and squeezed Phoebe's hand, and though the gesture wasn't sexual, he felt a definite throb in his groin. They remained that way a few minutes, fingers intertwined, communicating without words, much the way they used to.

"It hurts to think of you behind bars, too," she said again, so much pain in her words.

"Like I said, it forced me to grow up fast and to get my shit together. I can't say that would have happened otherwise. It brought me to Brent, who taught me everything I know. It's thanks to him that I have the chance at a solid future."

"Well, I'm glad. You deserved that."

He nodded. "How about we move on to lighter things? Tell me about how you got into real estate."

She lit up at the subject of her career, pulling her hand from his so she could gesture as she began to regale him with stories of some of the funnier clients she'd had, the odd list of requirements some people had when buying a house, and she exhibited pride when it came to some of her more recent, larger sales.

"One day I'd like to open my own office. Get away from Harvey, my boss," she said.

"What's wrong with him?"

She wrinkled her nose. "He's one of those men who makes you uncomfortable. He looks a little too long, doesn't know the meaning of personal space, you know?"

He narrowed his gaze, his temper rising over the fact that she'd been subjected to some asshole's bad behavior. "Did he touch you?" he asked, fingers curling into fists.

She shook her head. "It's all been subtle innuendo." She wrinkled her nose. "The man's a pig."

"Have you talked to anyone about it? An office manager? Someone?"

"No. He's the owner. There's no one to reprimand him, but relax. I can handle him."

He hated the fact that she worked somewhere where she was subjected to harassment. "You shouldn't have to put up with that."

"It is what it is." She shrugged, obviously unconcerned or at least used to it as a fact of life. "He owns the biggest real estate firm in the area. I'd be foolish to walk away."

"Until you go out on your own, you mean."

She grinned. "Maybe one day."

The rest of the meal passed easily between them, but underneath was a lingering sexual awareness that had been there through the entire dinner.

She declined dessert, saying she had to get home because she had an early showing in the morning.

He paid the check and walked her out to her car, his hand on the small of her back. Being with her again felt good. Catching up made it seem like he knew her again.

He felt like something important had been returned to him tonight, something he hadn't known he was missing until he'd gotten it back. Things between them definitely weren't over, and if he had his way, this night would be the first date of many.

PHOEBE WALKED OUT of the restaurant, Jake's hand on her back, a touch that felt more like a brand. So many times during dinner, in spite of the seriousness of the conversation, she'd felt of an undercurrent of sexual awareness burning bright between them, and she was certain he'd felt it, too.

"My car is over there." She pointed to her white vehicle parked beneath a light.

He guided her, pausing behind the trunk of her car.

"This was nice," she said. "Catching up and talking."

"I'd like to do it again," he said, his smile pure sin.

A ripple of awareness trickled through her veins. "Me, too. I have so much more to share with you," she murmured.

Dinner conversation had been heavy enough without her bringing up the fact that he had a son. Not to mention how public the restaurant had felt. But she was determined that he know and soon.

He leaned in closer and she trembled beneath the cooler air surrounding her.

"Tomorrow night?" he asked, pushing her for a fast second date.

Not that she'd thought this had been a date, but when it came to the two of them, the connection was obviously still strong.

"I can't tomorrow." She'd promised to host a sleepover for one of Jamie's friends.

"Next Friday then."

She laughed at his perseverance. "You're persistent."

"I am when I want something." He paused. "There's still something between us, Phoebe."

She looked into his eyes and nodded, unable to deny the obvious truth.

"I'll see you at the house during the week?" he asked.

"Yes." Maybe then she'd find time to talk to him with no one else around.

He leaned in and kissed her cheek, brushing his lips over her skin. He lingered, his breath warm on her flesh, causing her nipples to pucker beneath her dress. Her hand came up to cup his forearm, steadying herself against the sexual tension between them.

His lips trailed across her cheek, and when she turned her head a fraction, his lips brushed hers. His lips were warm, his kiss gentle and way too brief.

He pulled back, leaving her wanting so much more. "Good night, Phoebe," he said in a husky voice.

"Good night," she murmured. With trembling hands, she reached into her bag to retrieve her keys.

He held open her car door and waited for her to climb into her car and drive away. And as she watched him disappear in her rearview mirror, her heart pounded out a rapid beat, and excitement and panic warred for dominance inside her. Because somehow, in her effort to understand the man he'd become so she could decide whether to let her son know his father, she'd managed to complicate an already sticky situation.

UNABLE TO SLEEP, Phoebe sat on her back patio drinking a glass of white wine before bed. She'd needed to unwind after her dinner with Jake. After that kiss, so brief yet so intense. As serious as all the truths told and the confidences revealed tonight.

She needed to tell him soon. She couldn't use the he'd-been-in-prison excuse to keep him away from his child, not when he'd owned up to his past mistakes.

She took a sip of wine and stared up at the starry sky, thinking of Jake and the man he'd become. He was so straightforward, so down-to-earth and full of self-knowledge and understanding. As for his time behind bars, her heart hurt for him, knowing it hadn't been as easy as he'd led her to believe. Sure, it had led him to a better place, but the time there had to have been awful.

She admired his outlook, but the truth was she admired a lot more than what was inside him. He'd grown into himself physically. Handsome, dark hair, full lips. Broad shoulders, muscles in all the right places. And strong thighs. She knew because her own thighs had brushed with his during their dinner, and her entire body had sizzled at the hard touch of his leg against hers.

And when he'd leaned in and kissed her cheek and lingered before moving to her lips, she'd breathed in his masculine cologne and her nipples had hardened beneath the material of her dress.

But it was difficult to think of him as a man she desired when there was still so much emotional baggage between them. Not only did he have a child he didn't know about, he'd been married. She didn't know what he felt about his ex-wife, who'd wanted the divorce or why. What if he was still hung up on her? It would be foolish of Phoebe to want something that wasn't possible.

And besides, she had a little boy to consider. Just because she still felt something for Jake didn't mean she could act on it. After all, if he reciprocated and they got together but things didn't work out, her son would find himself in the middle of his parents and that wasn't fair.

Life would be complicated enough with Jamie getting to know his dad. Her own feelings and desires couldn't factor into the equation.

AFTER WORKING LONG hours that included Jake's crew beginning to freshen up the existing paint and moldings in the house, he called it a day. "Let's start again in the morning," he said to his men.

"Jake, what do you say we grab some dinner before we head home?" Gregg, his new foreman, asked.

Jake's stomach grumbled and he nodded. "Sounds good."

"One of the kitchen guys said there's a good pizza place in town. Want to try it?"

"Sure thing." The outside contractors had already finished and gone home, so Jake locked up the Renault place and followed Gregg by car into the town of Rosewood Bay.

The main street was an eclectic combination of storefronts, common to small, local beach towns, giving the area character instead of bland uniformity. Sal's Pizza was on the corner, located by the barbershop.

He parked and headed inside, the delicious smell of garlic assaulting his senses. He met up with Gregg, and they ordered a large pepperoni pizza and sodas, then headed to the back of the restaurant to find a table.

The place was fairly crowded. The noise level was high thanks to a video game in one corner and groups of kids with their friends and parents at various tables.

Jake chose a table by the wall and took a seat, his back to the rest of the room.

"Man, I'm hungry," Gregg said, sitting across from him.

"Same here. It's been a long time since lunch."

Gregg laughed. "Listen, I wanted to thank you again for the promotion. I'm sorry it came at JD's expense, but it's a great opportunity for me."

Jake inclined his head. "You earned the position." And he would have promoted him one way or another, never mind what his old foreman had done. "How's your wife?"

"Very pregnant," Gregg said with a shake of his head. "She's due soon. Another reason this promotion came at the right time."

They talked about the plans on the Renault place and other projects lined up for afterwards.

Jake glanced at his watch. "I'll go check on the pizza," he said. "Be right back." He rose and headed up front.

The guy behind the counter handed him the drinks and told him that he'd bring the pie back to his table as soon as it was ready.

As he was walking back into the crowded room, a woman stopped Jake, getting into his personal space. "I think you should be keeping an eye on your child," she said, pursing her lips in obvious annoyance.

He narrowed his gaze. "I'm not sure what you're talking about but—"

"I'm talking about your son spilling his drink and nobody being around to help."

Jake shook his head. "Ma'am, I'm bringing my drinks back for myself and a friend. I don't have a child here," he said, holding up the full cups in his hands.

She glanced at him, surprise etched on her features. "Oh! That boy looks just like you!" She pointed to a dark-haired boy who appeared about ten years old.

The child was wiping a spilled drink with a flimsy napkin, his cheeks bright red. He looked up and blue eyes just like Jake's stared back at him.

"Jesus."

"Jamie? What happened?" Phoebe's voice traveled toward him as he watched her rush over. "I went to the bathroom for two minutes!" She pulled desperately at the napkins in the dispenser on the table, trying to clean up the mess.

"Sorry to have bothered you," the woman who'd been lecturing him said.

Jake ignored her, his eyes on Phoebe and the ten-year-old boy... who looked just like Jake had at that age.

As if in slow motion, he made his way over to the

table, bracing a hand on the edge to steady himself. "Phoebe?"

She swung around at the sound of his voice, startled eyes meeting his. "Jake." All color drained from her face, answering any lingering doubt he might have had.

This boy was his son.

Chapter Four

"THIS IS A surprise." Jake managed to keep his voice level as he spoke, despite the dull roar in his ears that had nothing to do with the loud sounds in the restaurant.

"Who's that, Mom?" the boy asked.

Yeah, who was he? What was Phoebe going to say to their child? He met her gaze, unwilling to make this situation easier for her.

"Jamie, this is… this is an old friend of mine, Jake Nichols." She visibly swallowed hard, her face still pale. "Jake, this is my son, Jamie."

"Nice to meet you, Jamie." Willing his hand not to tremble, Jake held it out for the boy to take.

Unable to tear his gaze from his son's face, memorizing his features one by one, he shook the boy's hand, Jamie's palm sticky from the soda spill and subsequent cleanup attempt. The boy winced as they parted hands, the tackiness from the liquid obvious between them.

"Honey, go into the bathroom and wash up," Phoebe suggested. "I'll finish cleaning up here." She gestured to the restroom near the table where they sat.

Jamie disappeared behind the swinging door and Jake turned to her. "You had hours on Saturday night to tell me, Phoebe. What the fuck?"

"I… It isn't that simple. And this isn't something we can hash out here. Jamie's going to be back any minute."

Jake narrowed his gaze but knew she was right. "Make no mistake, Phoebe, we will discuss it and soon."

"I know," she said, tears in her eyes.

Tears because she'd never wanted him to find out? Or because she felt guilty for withholding the information? He didn't know but he felt physically ill.

"Hey, our pizza's ready," Gregg said, coming up behind Jake and tapping him on the shoulder.

"I'll be right there." He kept his gaze on Phoebe's. "When?" he asked, not letting her off the hook. "When can we talk about this?"

"Mom, is our food ready yet?" Jamie walked back to the table, talking as he approached.

"Soon, Jamie," she said, not breaking Jake's intense stare.

When she didn't give Jake a definite time, he took

control. "Tomorrow morning. Your place or mine, I don't care which," he said in a low voice.

"Mine," she said. "After I drop him off at school. Nine a.m.?"

"Text me the address."

She nodded, clearly still shaken up. He knew the feeling. His entire world had just been upended.

The guy from behind the front counter showed up just then with a pizza in hand. "Pepperoni pizza," he said, placing the tray down on the stand on the table.

"My favorite," Jamie said, a big grin on his face.

"Mine, too." Jake smiled at the boy who'd already begun to dig into a slice. "I wonder what else we have in common," he said to Phoebe.

A stricken look crossed her face. "I told you that I tried to find you, remember? I never planned to keep him away from you." She spoke low so Jamie wouldn't overhear.

"You just didn't mention it at the first opportunity."

Jake wasn't angry at her for the eleven years he'd missed, though he hated the fact that it had happened and would have to come to terms with it somehow. But he was damned disappointed in her for not enlightening him immediately.

He turned to the table and the boy devouring his dinner. "Nice to meet you, Jamie."

He glanced up, pizza in hand. "Thanks," he said over a mouthful of food.

"Swallow before speaking," Phoebe said, in mom mode. "Then say good-bye to Mr.—"

She caught Jake's glare and cleared her throat.

"Say good-bye to Jake," she said, before turning to face Jake alone. "I'll make this right," she whispered.

"Damn right you will, because I need to know my son. And he needs to know me."

PHOEBE WAS FRANTIC, and as soon as she'd gotten Jamie to sleep, she called her sister, needing someone to talk to. Or more like she needed someone to listen.

"I'm freaking out," she said to her sister, pacing the deck, enjoying her favorite spot of the house.

"Calm down. You knew you'd be telling him eventually," Halley said in a soothing tone.

Phoebe placed one hand on the stone pillar in the corner of the patio. "It's not so much that he knows about Jamie as it is what it means. I have to tell Jamie about his dad, and that means life as I know it is about to change and I'm not ready. I thought I was, but it'll mean sharing, and for so long it's been me and Jamie. Just us. And you guys, but you know what I mean. God, I'm rambling." She let out a shaky laugh.

"Breathe deep," her sister ordered in a firm tone.

"I don't want you hyperventilating."

"Okay. Okay." Phoebe breathed in and out a few times, taking in slow, steady streams of air. "It's not that I didn't know these things, but considering them in the abstract is one thing and facing them in reality is so much harder."

"Tackle things one at a time," Halley suggested. "First you need to talk to Jake. Then you'll have to tell Jamie. After that, they'll need to meet. He's not going to run off with Jamie or take him away before both of you are ready."

"I might never be ready!" she practically wailed.

"Shh. Do you want me to come over?" her sister offered.

Phoebe sniffed and wiped a tear from her eye. "No, I'll be okay." She had no choice but to pull herself together.

"I know you will be. You're strong. You can do this."

She straightened her shoulders. "You're right. He looked so hurt," she said, hitting on the other thing that had been bothering her.

"Phoebe, you didn't tell him in the week since you've seen him again. It's not like you held out for years. He'll get over the shock."

"You're right," Phoebe said again. She was torturing herself over too many things. She just had to let the situation play out, as Halley had suggested. "When did you become so wise?" she asked her younger sister.

Halley let out a laugh. "We're all wise about things that don't impact our own lives. Remember what a mess I was about Kane?"

The memory made Phoebe smile, not because her sister had almost lost the man she loved but because it reminded Phoebe that everyone felt insecure and crazy sometimes.

This was just her time.

JAKE WENT FROM Sal's Pizza to his mother's in Thornton. He'd grown up in this house, with her strength and wisdom to guide him, and he'd taken it for granted, not recognizing the value of what he had. He was grateful she was still there for him now.

She was youthful-looking, her dark hair hanging loose about her shoulders, her eyes the same blue as his... and Jamie's.

"What brings you by so late?" his mother asked.

"I have a son," he said to his mother, unable to hide his excitement, not to mention his ongoing shock.

"What? What do you mean? Callie's a girl, and well, I don't understand!"

He detailed his time with Phoebe when he was

young, how he'd run into her again last week, had a catch-up dinner this past Saturday, and discovered he was a father—again—earlier this evening.

"Oh my! Jake!" His mother stared at him with wide eyes. "That means I have another grandchild."

"And Callie has a brother." There was so much to consider, Jake's head was spinning.

"Come sit and stop pacing."

He turned and walked to where she sat on her sofa in the family room.

He settled in beside her, in need of her wisdom now more than ever. "How do I walk in to the life of an eleven-year-old?" he asked. "Will he want to know me? Or will he resent me for not being there all these years?"

She shook her head and placed her hand over his. "He's going to be happy to have you in his life," she assured him. "I'm not saying it won't take some adjustment, but that's only to be expected."

"I'm more nervous than when I was before Callie was born. How is that possible?" he asked, his stomach threatening to rebel against the pizza he'd eaten earlier.

"It's normal, I'm sure. But Jake, you know what you're doing. You're a wonderful father to Callie. You and Lindsay manage to co-parent quite well."

At the mention of his ex, Jake froze. "Oh shit.

Lindsay."

"Language," his mom said like she used to when he was younger.

He laughed. "Sorry, Mom, but seriously. Lindsay is going to go crazy when she finds out I have a child with another woman."

His ex had never stopped treating him as hers despite the divorce. Because he'd never dated a woman who mattered, he hadn't had cause to put a stop to the behavior, but it was out of control, as he'd told her the other day. If she thought her position was threatened, she'd lose her mind.

She patted his hand. "You can handle Lindsay. You always have. Now when can I meet my grandson?"

He chuckled. "I'll let you know once I do." From the panicked look on Phoebe's face, he had a hunch he was looking at a slow process, which he respected. If it were Callie and the situation were reversed, he'd have reservations of his own. He'd let Phoebe dictate the rules as long as they were within reason.

But first he wanted to understand where her head was when it came to him. Why she hadn't just told him when they were alone together on Saturday and what that meant for them going forward.

✧   ✧   ✧

JAKE ARRIVED AT the address Phoebe texted him, prepared to talk but completely unprepared for the mansion that greeted him as he approached. Apparently when Phoebe was *rescued* from foster care, it'd been by a *wealthy* aunt. She'd neglected to mention that fact.

She had told him to drive past the main house to a guesthouse behind it, and he did as instructed, parking in front of the overly large house that also blew him away. Clearly there was a lot he didn't know about Phoebe.

He parked and walked up to the front door, ringing the bell at exactly nine a.m., his heart pounding hard inside his chest. Although he wasn't going to see his son, he damned well was going to arrange a time for that introduction, father to son this time, no matter what Phoebe might think.

She opened the door wearing her business suit and hair pulled back into a bun, which he took to mean she wanted to keep things distant between them. To hell with that, he thought, wanting to talk to the woman behind the professional armor she wore.

"Hi," she said.

"Morning. Nice place," he said, gesturing with a hand to the grounds that surrounded them.

She bit down on her lower lip before answering. "Thank you. My aunt owns the property and I pay rent here," she said, obviously seeing the need for explanation. "Come on in. We can talk in the living room."

She led him through a hallway with framed photographs on one wall, pictures of Jamie as a baby, toddler, and various stages of growing up. Jake paused to take them all in, to see what he'd missed out on. From the first squishy baby picture to the photos of a little boy with missing teeth, Jake took in the stages of his son's life, hurting for what might have been had life been different. Phoebe remained silent beside him, letting him look his fill.

Finally he turned, ready to walk away from the montage on the wall. He followed her to a large living room with French doors overlooking a patio with an extraordinary view of the landscape beyond.

"This must have taken getting used to," he said. "Coming from foster care."

She nodded. "It was an adjustment, to say the least, but I found out I was pregnant pretty soon after I moved into the main house. I didn't have time to dwell on where I was living. I just knew I was fortunate to be somewhere where I had support and not with a family that might throw me out the second they discovered I was having a baby." She settled into the sofa, patting the seat beside her.

He took the cue and sat down where she'd gestured. "Your aunt was supportive?" he asked, knowing it must have been a difficult situation. One he'd missed out on. "She didn't want you to... I don't know. Put the baby up for adoption or have an abortion?" The words made him nauseous. "I mean, you were all of sixteen years old."

She glanced down at her hands. "She laid out all my options, including keeping the baby. She made it clear it was my decision and she'd be there for me no matter what I decided." A small smile lifted her lips as she looked at him. "She was really good to me."

"Except she didn't want you to have anything to do with me," he said, aware his tone was full of resentment. "You said she found me? And decided not to tell you."

She expelled a harsh breath. "Yes. She made that choice for me. She said it was because you were in prison for assault, that she didn't think that bringing you into the situation was the right thing for me or the baby." She choked on her words, her eyes filling with tears. "I'm sorry. It wasn't her decision to make."

Her remorse and the fact that she didn't agree with her aunt's decision helped the pain inside him. She hadn't had the right to make that choice, but she'd been in control of the situation. Neither he nor Phoebe could change the past now.

And there was a part of him that didn't blame the woman for the decision she'd made. All she'd known was that Phoebe's baby's father was a loser in prison, doing time for a violent crime. He winced as the truth rolled through him.

It wasn't the first time he'd thought that about himself, but this was the first time his choices had hurt more than him. It'd hurt Phoebe, who'd had his baby and raised him without a father, and it had hurt Jake's son.

"I'm sorry I wasn't there for you," he said, his voice breaking. And knowing her aunt hadn't thought he was good enough for Phoebe or his own child burned a hole inside him. But could he blame her?

"It wasn't your fault," she whispered.

But they both knew it was.

He wondered what her aunt thought about him now that he was back in Phoebe's life. He didn't want to care, but something told him the woman had a profound influence and place in both Phoebe's and his son's life. What kind of obstacle would she prove to be, if any? he wondered, then decided he'd just worry about it when the time came.

He looked at Phoebe, who appeared sad but composed. More pulled together than he felt at the moment.

"Let's move on," he said gruffly. "Why the hell didn't you tell me? You had time when you came to see the Renault house and while we were confiding in each other Saturday night. I don't fucking understand.

Were you planning on keeping him from me?"

"God, no." Her eyes opened wide in horror and he saw the truth there. "I just… At first it was a shock to see you. I needed to process that you were back in my life, what it would mean for me, for Jamie. Then I found out about your time in jail, and though I knew in my heart there had to be a good reason, I needed to understand what had happened before I let you around my son."

She reached out and grabbed his hand and he took strength in her touch. "I hadn't seen you in over a decade, Jake. You had a temper back then. What kind of mother would I be if I didn't look out for my son?"

Not a good one, he thought, lowering his shoulders as he acknowledged her words, ashamed of who he'd been. "I get it. But after I explained the circumstances, you seemed to understand. Why didn't you tell me then?"

She swallowed hard. "Everything we talked about that night was so heavy and deep. I didn't want to add to it. And we were surrounded by people. I told myself I could tell you the next time we were alone, but maybe I was justifying it to myself because I was nervous. I don't know. But I swear to you it was never my plan to keep Jamie a secret or withhold him from you."

"Okay," he said, accepting her at her word. "So

where do we go from here?"

"I've asked myself that same question over and over," she admitted.

Jake frowned at that. "I want him to know I'm his father." No ifs, ands, or buts about that.

She visibly swallowed hard, and though he respected her nervousness, he wasn't caving on this.

"I know," she said with a nod of agreement. "What about your little girl? How are you going to handle that?" she asked, biting down on her lower lip.

"Callie's sweet and easy. She'll be fine. She's young enough to make an easy adjustment." Unlike his ex, who was going to freak. Not just because he had a child but because he had one with Phoebe, the woman she'd always sensed he'd never gotten over.

But he wasn't going to bring his issues with Lindsay into his relationship with Phoebe. He had enough between them to worry about. "When the time is right for Jamie, I'll introduce them."

Phoebe relaxed her shoulders. Obviously the subject had been weighing on her. "So I guess the next step is me telling Jamie about you."

"I was hoping to be there." It was a big pronouncement and he wanted his son to know that though he might have missed way too much before now, from this point forward, Jake was all in.

She shook her head. "I want him to feel free to

react how he wants to react… and if you're there, he might not be comfortable doing that."

He bit down on the inside of his cheek. "I can handle his reaction."

"But maybe he can't deal with his own emotions. He's an eleven-year-old boy. He could be excited, which is the best-case scenario, or he could be angry at time missed, and in that eventuality, I don't want him to hurt your feelings." She placed her hand on his. "Let me be the buffer? Please? Let me take the brunt of his reaction, good or bad, before bringing the two of you together."

He exhaled a hard breath, knowing he was going to give in. "You're his mother. You know what's best for him," he said, hating the fact that he didn't know Jamie at all.

"Thank you!" Her shoulders slumped, her relief palpable, as she flung her arms around his neck and pulled him to her in thanks.

He hugged her back, inhaled her fragrant scent, and suddenly his body forgot about everything else on his mind. When he was holding her like this, there was just them and how right she felt in his arms. His cock throbbed in agreement.

Down, boy, he thought, knowing this wasn't the time. But he promised himself that when things settled with Jamie, he would make the time to get to know her again. To bring them closer in every way possible.

Chapter Five

PHOEBE WAITED UNTIL the weekend, not wanting Jamie to be distracted by school when she told him the news. She cooked his favorite meal, lasagna, and let him have Coke with dinner, softening him up and wanting him to be happy before she altered his world forever.

The fact was, this would be good for Jamie, once he digested the information. No more Father's Day sadness. No more father-son breakfasts at school that he begged to miss. This was a good thing, something she'd once prayed could happen.

She just needed to sit him down and tell him the news.

She finished cleaning the kitchen and called him from his room, where he was busy with his X-Box.

"Mom, let me finish this game," he yelled back.

"Come on, bud. I need to talk to you," she returned.

She heard him putting down the console and stomping down the hall. With his size sevens, she always heard him coming. More like a herd of cattle than one little man.

He entered the den, where she sat on the couch. "Come sit," she said, patting the sofa.

He skidded to a halt beside her and dropped onto the cushion. "What's up?" he asked, looking at her with curious blue eyes.

With his father's eyes.

"Listen… do you remember that I once told you I tried to find your dad?"

His shocked gaze came to hers. He hadn't expected this topic of conversation. "Yeah. But he was sent away by the state and you lost track of him."

Her smart boy remembered everything she'd told him about his father.

"Well, sometimes fate steps in and brings people back to you."

He looked at her funny. "I'm confused."

She laughed. Right. Of course he was confused because she was beating around the point. "I ran into your dad, honey. I hadn't seen him for years, and then I walked into a house to meet a contractor and there he was."

"You saw my dad?" he asked, his voice rising.

She nodded. Swallowed hard. She took his hand,

which was so big now, and held on. "And so did you. Remember the man from the pizza place? Jake Nichols?"

Her son nodded, eyes wide.

"Well, he's your father. I was surprised to see him there, too. And I didn't want to spring it on you in public. And I hadn't told him about you yet. So I needed to talk to you both alone."

She was rambling to her eleven-year-old.

She pulled herself together. "Do you understand what I'm telling you?"

"That man I met… he's my dad?"

She nodded.

"Does he know about me yet?" he asked, sounding more like an uncertain little boy than he had in a while.

Her heart squeezed as she answered. "Not only does he know but he's dying to… well re-meet you, this time as your father." She waited a beat, then asked, "How do you feel about that?"

He kicked his bare feet against the hardwood floor. His smelly bare feet. But she needed to wait before getting on him about a shower.

"Do you want to see him?" she asked.

"Does he really want to see me?"

"Oh, honey. He really does. I had to ask him to let me tell you by myself. He wanted to be here so badly."

He shrugged. "Then yeah. I want to see him, too,"

he said, trying to sound cool when she could tell he was vibrating with excitement, his body practically shaking.

She grinned. "Is tomorrow too soon? Because I have to call and let him know and he's going to want to do it soon."

"Yeah, that's good," he said, suddenly sounding uncertain.

"What's wrong?" She put a hand on his shoulder. "You can talk to me."

He looked up at her from beneath thick lashes. "What if he doesn't like me?"

Her throat filled at the fragile question. "What's not to like?" she asked, nudging him with her elbow. "You're smart, you're friendly, you're a good kid with a big heart. Come on. He's going to love you." She pulled him into her arms, grateful he was still young enough to accept her motherly affection.

She dreaded the day he pulled away from her and she'd have to let him go. "You have nothing to worry about," she promised him, and because she knew what an upstanding man his dad was, she was certain she could trust in her own words.

✧　✧　✧

JAKE LEANED BACK in his bed, his shirt off, wearing only a pair of boxer briefs as he relaxed before bed.

His phone rang and he glanced at the screen, surprised when Phoebe's name flashed on the screen. He answered immediately. "Hi," he said.

"Hi. So I wanted to tell you that I told Jamie about you tonight," she said, obviously speaking quietly into the phone, her voice a husky sound that, despite the seriousness of the subject, went straight to his groin.

"How'd he take it?" he asked, holding his breath.

"Really well. He's excited to see you again."

Relief flooded through him. "That's great."

"Yes. But he's nervous, Jake. He's wondering if you're going to like him," she said, clearly prepping him for what to expect.

Jake let out a rough laugh. "I've been worried about the same thing."

"He's a good kid. You have nothing to worry about," she reassured him.

"What did you tell him about me?" he asked, curious.

"What do you think? That you're a good man and you're going to love him."

"Do you really believe that? That I'm a good man?" Sometimes, in the dead of night, when prison crept up on him and his past closed in, he wasn't so sure.

"I wouldn't lie to my son. And if I didn't think that, I wouldn't let you get near him, regardless of the fact that you're his father." Her voice sounded warm and calm in his ear.

Silence echoed between them but it wasn't uncomfortable at all. "I missed you, you know. After we were separated, I thought about you all the time," he couldn't help but tell her.

She sighed. "Me, too. And after I found out I was pregnant, I wanted you with me so badly."

"I'm sorry," he said gruffly. "We were too fucking young. I wish I could change the past."

"Not all of it," she said. "Not what we meant to each other. And not Jamie."

His heart thumped hard in his chest. "No, none of that. You got me through it, you know. Thinking of you and the times we spent together, I was able to leave my body and pretend I was somewhere else. With you."

"Jake," she said, her voice cracking.

He didn't want her to be sad. "It's all good now. We're going to make up for lost time."

"You and Jamie are, yes."

He closed his eyes against those words. Because when he thought about his future, he was beginning to believe he wanted her in it. Too soon to think that way? Probably. But now that she was back in his life, he didn't think he could let her go again.

✧　✧　✧

NERVES ABOUT MEETING Jamie again kept Jake up most of the night, and by the time he walked into Phoebe's house the next day, he was strung tight. He did his best to keep his body and facial expression relaxed, not wanting to scare Jamie because he looked too serious or intense.

He followed Phoebe into the den, where Jamie waited. He sat on the couch, almost the spitting image of Jake when he was a boy.

"Hi," Jake said, sitting on the couch not too close so as not to overwhelm him.

"Hi." Jamie glanced down, shyer than when they'd met at the pizza place with sticky soda hands between them.

Jake was at a loss and glanced at Phoebe, silently asking for help.

"Why don't you tell Jake about baseball," she suggested to Jamie. "Jamie plays in the town league."

"Yeah? What position?" Jake asked.

Jamie still didn't look Jake in the eye as he said, "Left field."

"Do you like it?"

He shrugged. "Sometimes, I need practice. Coach says it'll help my skills but I don't get much chance."

Jake didn't know what to make of his answer. Once again, he glanced at Phoebe.

"I'm not much of a sports person," she said from

where she stood watching them. "Kane works with him when he can, but the garage has been busy lately and he hasn't been able to take the time off."

"Kane?" he asked, wondering about this other man in her and his son's life.

"Halley's boyfriend. They've been together almost a year. He's been great, stepping in when he can. But there's just us women in the family otherwise. Until now."

He breathed a groan of relief that there was no man with whom he had to vie for Phoebe's and his son's attention.

As for baseball, although Jake didn't want to push, he saw an opening with which he could get to know his son better. "If you like, I can come by and we could throw the ball, practice a little?" he offered.

The first glimmer of interest sparkled in Jamie's gaze. "You'd do that?"

"Sure thing. If it's okay with your mom, we can go outside in a little while."

He glanced over to see Phoebe smiling at the suggestion.

"What's your favorite team?" he asked Jamie. "I'm a Yankees fan, myself."

"Me, too!" he said excitedly, a grin on his face.

They spent the next few minutes talking about favorite players before Jamie asked, "Can we go outside now? Please, Mom? I need to practice and ... *he* said he'd play catch with me. Please?"

Jake caught the boy's stumbling over what to call Jake and his heart gave a small squeeze. He knew it was too soon for Jamie to call him Dad, but with everything in him, he hoped for the chance.

"Jamie, why don't you go get changed to play outside. I want to talk to Jake for a few minutes."

"Okay." He ran to his room, leaving them alone.

Phoebe turned to Jake. "Are you okay?" she asked.

"A little shaky," he said honestly, his stomach still in knots over the meeting. He'd wanted so badly for Jamie to like him. "It's not every day you fumble for conversation with a son you barely know."

"Well, sports is the great equalizer." She smiled at him, obviously pleased with how this first meeting had gone. "He's nervous, too, remember? Just be yourself. It'll get easier over time," she assured him.

He nodded at her certainty. "You've done a good job with him, Phoebe."

Her cheeks flushed pink. "Thank you. I can't say it's always been easy, but he's such a good kid, he makes it simpler."

Needing to be closer to her, he walked over to where she stood. He didn't know how to broach the subject on his mind other than to just spit it out. "I want to be there for him, and for you, from now on.

In reality as well as helping out financially."

Another thing he'd given a lot of thought to since finding out he had a son. He made a very good living with Brent, and he didn't live expensively. But he paid spousal and child support to Lindsay. While she had stayed in the small house they'd bought as their starter home, he'd taken a reasonably priced apartment with enough room for his daughter to stay over. Jamie could sleep there if he ever stayed over, but if Callie were there, too, Jake had a pullout sofa that he could use. But he was getting ahead of himself. For now he just had to worry about re-budgeting so he could pay his share for his son, too.

She blinked, clearly startled by his proclamation. "I... Well ... we can discuss things," she said hesitantly.

He leaned a hip against the back edge of the sofa. "Talk to me. What are you thinking?"

She met his gaze. "My pride wants to tell you I can handle it, but my common sense says you're his father and I should let you help."

"You're honest as well as pragmatic and I respect that. But your common sense is right. It's my pleasure as well as my responsibility. We can work out specifics another time."

"Okay." She inclined her head. "Umm, do you want to stay for dinner?" she asked.

"Thanks, but no. I think I should go easy. I don't want to overwhelm Jamie with my presence. We can set up another time for me to see him and go from there."

She nodded. "Sounds good."

"That takes care of me and Jamie, but what about me and you?"

She wrinkled her nose in confusion.

"Me finding out put a wrinkle in our plans to go out for dinner. You owe me a date," he said in a low voice because he heard drawers opening and closing from Jamie's room, reminding him they weren't alone.

"I wasn't thinking clearly when I agreed to go out with you again. We have Jamie to worry about."

"I don't think he'd mind his parents sharing a meal." He brushed her hair off her shoulders, threading the soft strands through his fingers. "I'm not going to take no for an answer because you already indicated you want to go out with me again."

She trembled beneath his featherlight touch. "I just think we should be smart."

"And we will be."

He just wasn't willing to sacrifice them for the sake of problems that weren't there.

WITH THE WEEKEND behind her, Phoebe walked into

the real estate office on Monday morning, planning to do some paperwork before she had a showing later today. She looked through the daily hot sheet, familiarizing herself with information on new listings, price changes on properties, etc. She pulled listings to show today's clients, a couple with a pregnant wife who was looking to upgrade their current rental apartment to their first home.

She headed into the break room to get a cup of coffee and ran into the owner, Harvey Walsh, a man she usually tried to avoid being alone with.

"Good morning, Phoebe." He turned from the coffeemaker to face her, then looked her over, his gaze leering as he stared, from her bare legs in her suit to her chest where her camisole parted beneath the jacket.

She deliberately didn't react to his perusal, not wanting him to have the satisfaction of knowing he made her uneasy. "Good morning, Harvey. How was your weekend with Renee?" she asked of his wife, deliberately inserting her name into the conversation. As a reminder that he was married. And even if he wasn't, he was still crossing a line in the workplace.

"We had a very nice weekend. Thank you." He stepped into her space, his big body too close to hers. "And that's a lovely suit you're wearing. It shows your figure quite nicely."

She stiffened, this time unable to hold back her reaction. "I think I'll get my coffee later," she said, spinning around and heading back to her desk, heart pounding harder than normal.

She tried to concentrate but couldn't focus, not after her boss had been so blatant in his inspection of her clothes and body. Instead of doing more paperwork, she gathered her things and headed out for the day, planning to stop at Celeste's house before her afternoon showings.

She told herself she needed to check on progress, but the truth was, she wanted to see Jake. She hadn't been able to stop thinking of him since Saturday, when he'd come to see Jamie. The meeting between them had gone well, Jamie turning into his shy, introspective self around his newfound father. But at the mention of baseball and at the idea of practicing, her son had lit up.

He and Jake had spent an hour outside, Jake giving Jamie pointers on how to throw and catch, and doing it in a way that had built up Jamie's ego, not tearing it down when he missed or performed incorrectly. Her heart had warmed watching them, the excitement on Jamie's face when he did something new or correctly and the awe on Jake's that he'd reached the boy. For the rest of the weekend, all she'd heard from Jamie was *Jake said this* or *Jake did that*, she thought with a grin.

She'd also spent the rest of the weekend contemplating Jake's offer to help financially. The fact was, Phoebe had had a recent high-end sale that put her into a very comfortable position. Jamie didn't want for anything, and she was able to pay her aunt a fair amount of rent, not that Joy needed or wanted the money. It was Phoebe's pride that demanded she stand on her own.

But with Jake's help, she could start putting money away for college for Jamie. She didn't know what he earned, but she was sure he paid for his daughter's support, and then there was his ex-wife. He probably also paid money there. She hoped this situation wasn't squeezing him too tight, but he hadn't given her any indication there were issues. It was for him to figure out, she told herself.

As for Jamie, and her accepting money, there would be luxuries he wanted for his birthday and next Christmas, and she wouldn't have to be as careful with her choices. He was his father, after all, and even Halley thought she should accept his offer.

Phoebe hadn't seen Aunt Joy since she'd found out she'd lied to her about Jake's whereabouts when she was a teenager. She'd forgiven her aunt immediately, knowing she only had Phoebe's best interests at heart, but that didn't mean there wasn't some lingering resentment there for the years her son had missed out on with his father. And for the time Jake had missed, as well.

And for what might have been between Jake and Phoebe as a couple. After all, they'd been in love when they'd been separated. What would have happened between them had he come back into her life? After he was let out of prison, would they have picked up where they left off before he'd met his ex-wife?

She shook her head, knowing the futility of wondering or changing the past. She had the present to deal with, and in the present, Jake wanted to get to know her again. And despite the pragmatic part of her that worried about her relationship with Jake affecting their son, her heart wanted to take a chance.

PHOEBE WALKED INTO Celeste's house to find Jake painting the chair rail in the entryway. "Hey there," he said, glancing up at her, looking sexy in his black tee shirt and paint-stained jeans. Jeans that hugged his hips and cradled the bulge in the front of the denim.

He put the paintbrush in the can and walked over to greet her. "I didn't think you were coming by today. But I'm glad you did," he said, a welcoming smile on his face.

"I needed to get out of my office." Her voice

trembled because no matter how hard she tried not to think about it, she was still shaken by how uncomfortable Harvey had made her.

"What's wrong?" Jake grabbed her hand in his and she took comfort in his strong, reassuring touch.

She met his gaze. "Nothing I can't handle. Just my boss looking me over like he had every right to inspect my body." She shivered in disgust.

"That's it," he said, sounding pissed, his sudden anger reminding her of when he was young and impulsive. "Someone needs to have a talk with that entitled asshole." Jake's ire was obvious, bubbling up and coming to the surface, all in her defense.

She placed a hand on his forearm to calm him down, his muscles jumping beneath her touch. "Jake, please. I need to work there. I can't go starting trouble." Nor could she have him stepping in for her.

Besides, he had a record and he could not get into a fight with Harvey, no matter how much she liked the thought of the man being pushed into a corner himself.

"You can damn well start trouble if he crosses the line, and he's fucking crossed it," Jake muttered.

She squeezed his arm tighter, his muscles hard beneath her fingers. "I really can deal with him. Today I just thought it was better to walk away."

He swore beneath his breath. "If he touches you

or it gets worse, I want to know about it."

"Are you my guardian?" she quipped, trying to keep things light as she tipped her head slightly, studying his tight, serious expression.

"I want to be." His voice was serious as hell.

His tone rubbed her in the most intimate way, her body swaying toward him. "Jake."

He reached out a hand to cup her face, his calloused fingertips rough against her skin. So intense were his features, so erotic was his touch, his protectiveness cloaking her in heat. Her nipples even puckered into tight points of need.

"If I had my way, nobody would be able to take advantage of you, because they'd have to go through me in order to get to you."

Her face warmed at his words. "That's sweet of you to say."

"I'm not feeling very sweet. In fact, I'm feeling pretty damned protective."

He was, and she liked it. A lot.

His fingers skimmed her cheek as he spoke. "I was lucky enough to find you again. I want a chance to see what could be between us," he said, taking her off guard.

But God, she wanted that, too. Despite her brain telling her they needed to tread carefully, that they had a little boy to protect, her traitorous heart still wanted more.

His blue gaze bored into hers, causing her heart to pound hard in her chest. "I know things are complicated right now, but how many people get second chances?"

"Not many," she agreed, knowing how lucky they were.

"So wouldn't we be foolish to waste the opportunity?"

She sighed, unable to argue with his words. "I want the chance, but I'm worried about all the things that could go wrong." Their son, his daughter, and his ex-wife, who Phoebe still didn't know enough about. Why had they broken up and what was their real relationship like now?

"Let me worry for both of us."

She wished she could do as he asked, but her makeup was to plan ahead and only do the smart thing, the right thing for her son.

"Now, what are your plans this weekend?"

She was relieved he'd let the subject of *them* go. "I promised Jamie we could go to the beach." She hesitated, then said, "Do you want to come with us?" It would be a great opportunity for Jamie to get to know his father and vice versa.

His eyes lit up at the invitation. "I'd love that. I was supposed to have Callie this weekend, but Lindsay asked if she could take her to her mom's, so I'm free. She said I could have a night during the week to make up for it."

And there was one of their potential obstacles. "Does Lindsay know about Jamie?" Phoebe asked.

He shook his head. "I was going to tell her when I picked up Callie, but since she canceled, I have to wait. I think telling her in person is the right thing to do."

She appreciated that he cared about his ex's feelings enough to respect *how* he informed her of this major life change.

"I agree," Phoebe said. "In person is the smartest way."

"Can I pick up you and Jamie for the beach on Saturday? I'm assuming you have a place in mind?"

She nodded. "There's a public stretch of beach I was planning to go to. You can come by at nine? I want to get a spot before it gets too crowded."

He grinned, obviously pleased to be able to spend the day with them.

Not as happy as she was to be with him.

Chapter Six

S ATURDAY DAWNED BRIGHT and sunny, a warm summer morning, perfect to spend at the beach. School had ended the day before, so Jamie was in an exceptionally good mood, looking forward to seeing friends and to spending the day with Jake.

At nine a.m. sharp, Jake arrived, wearing a pair of navy board shorts and a gray tee shirt and a pair of sunglasses, giving him a sexy look. Phoebe couldn't tear her gaze from his body, well-toned from manual labor.

She'd chosen a one-piece that went straight across her chest, no ties, with side cutouts, deferring to the mother in her but still wanting to look good when Jake saw her in a swimsuit for the first time.

They headed off together, Jake making conversation with Jamie about the end of school and his summer plans, which included day camp during the week and a lot of swimming on the weekends at his aunt's pool behind the main house. Jake didn't let conversation lapse, obviously over the worry of what to say to his son, and Phoebe was able to sit back and relax while the two developed a rapport of their own.

A little while later, they were set up on towels, relaxing on soft sand.

"Mom! I see Matthew! Can I go play?" Jamie gestured to where another family had spread their things out on a large blanket.

She glanced at Jake for approval to let Jamie go off with a friend, knowing he'd come here to see his son.

He gave her a quick nod and an understanding smile.

"Go ahead," she told him. "Just check in with me and don't go far."

"Mom!" He rolled his eyes at her overprotectiveness but that was too bad. It came with the mother territory. She laughed as he ran off with his friend.

"So much for quality time," she said, meeting Jake's gaze.

"It's fine. I just want him to have fun."

She reached into her beach bag and pulled out some sunscreen, then began applying it, aware of Jake's gaze on her as she slid her hands up and down her arms and legs, rubbing in the white lotion.

"Need help?" he asked.

"Sure. Get my back?" She handed him the bottle

and turned away, sliding her hair off her neck.

His big hand brushed the cool lotion on her neck, rubbing it into her skin before he moved on to her shoulders. The glide of his fingers felt good against her flesh, and she stifled a moan at the sensations that rushed through her courtesy of his touch.

His hands slid down to the cutouts in the sides of her swimsuit, his fingers easing over her bare flesh, working their way forward until he slipped his fingers around the front opening.

She sucked in a shallow breath at his teasing touch, the jolt of awareness going straight to body parts she shouldn't be aware of on the beach. Her nipples tightened, desire sliding its way to her sex. She shifted on the blanket, only succeeding in rubbing her thighs together and making herself even more aware of the man behind her.

"I think that covers everything," he said in a gruff voice.

"Yes. It certainly does." She took the bottle back from him, flipped the top closed, and stuffed it into her bag.

"What about me?" he asked. "Aren't you going to get my back?"

She swallowed hard, wary of running her hands along his bare skin. "Sure." She retrieved the bottle and poured some lotion into her hand.

He turned his back to her and she came face-to-face with his tanned, muscular frame. She rubbed her hands together and began to massage the lotion into his skin, feeling the hard stretch of muscles across his back and arms flexing beneath her fingertips.

"Damn, that feels good." The low growl in his voice sent ripples of awareness throughout her veins.

He waited until she finished, then turned to face her. A glance down and she realized he was just as affected as she was, his erection tenting his shorts. He cleared his throat and lifted one leg, blocking others from viewing his state of arousal.

Grinning at her, he shrugged, not embarrassed in the least. "What can I say? You get to me."

She blushed but admitted her own truth. "You get to me, too."

"Now that's a damn good thing to know." Jake began to reach for her.

"Mom!"

Jamie's voice broke into the heated moment and she guiltily glanced away. "What's up?" she asked her son.

Jamie was bouncing in front of her oversized beach towel. "Matthew's mom invited me to come home with them and have a sleepover. She said to ask you. And guess what? They got a puppy!"

She knew any chance of them having a family-like

day was shot now that a puppy was involved. "I can take you over there later," she told him, hoping to buy some time for him with Jake.

He looked upset, pouting like the boy he was. "But they have to leave soon because Rover needs to be walked and fed. They said I can come with them. Can I, Mom? Please?"

She sighed, torn, but she didn't think forcing him to hang out with the grown-ups was fair in the summertime, especially with a dog as a lure. "Sure, honey. Say good-bye to Jake," she told him.

He looked at his father. "Bye," he said shyly, ducking his head and running off once more.

She glanced regretfully at Jake. "Well, so much for a day at the beach."

"I'm not complaining." He propped himself up on one elbow. "I had a great conversation with my son earlier today, the sun is out now, and the company is good. What else could I ask for?"

She nearly melted under his intense gaze. "If you're happy, I'm happy. Let's enjoy." She lay back on the towel, allowing the sun to bake on her face. Except she couldn't stop feeling like he was watching her.

Opening her eyes, she turned to find his gaze steady on hers.

"This is the answer to my dreams," he said, and her mouth went dry. "I just never thought it would be my reality. That you could be my reality."

"Jake," she whispered, his words going straight to her heart because she'd often thought the same thing. She'd hoped to see him again, but she never thought they would be together.

But here they were.

"Jamie's with a friend, right?" he asked.

She nodded.

"Come home with me later," he said, his tone husky and filled with desire.

JAKE KNEW HE was moving quickly, but so much time had passed, could there really be such a thing as too much, too soon? He didn't think so, and when Phoebe put her hand in his, his heart kicked into high gear. Everything he wanted was within reach.

During the car ride over, he'd had his son talking to him like he was already a part of his life, filling him in on the last day of school and his baseball practice, no awkwardness to be found. The only thing missing was Callie, and he intended to integrate her very soon, introduce her to her new brother, and begin spending time with his son alone and as a family.

And then there was Phoebe, the woman he'd never gotten over, now wary but apparently willing to give *them* a try, which was the answer to every prayer he'd had since foster care.

After he suggested they return to his place, neither of them had been able to relax and enjoy the sun. As if on the same page, they cleaned up their beach area, tossing Jamie's things into her bag and rolling up the towels, their sole focus on being alone.

The ride to his apartment was quiet, the hum of sexual tension ever present between them. And by the time he opened the door to his apartment and let them inside, he was ready to devour her.

The door slammed shut and he turned to face her.

She'd covered that sexy swimsuit with a lace cover-up. Grasping the hem, he pulled it over her head, then backed her against the nearest wall and sealed his lips over hers.

Kissing her was like coming home, revisiting the best piece of his past and the most exciting part of his future. He slid his lips back and forth over hers before gliding his tongue into the deep recesses of her mouth. With a moan, she tangled her tongue with his. He cupped her face in his hands, holding her in place while he took what he wanted, giving back at the same time.

She trembled in his arms, and he slid a hand up the open cutout of her bathing suit, gliding his fingers beneath the material to skim the underside of her breast. Her hips arched against his, her needy sex skimming the hardness of his cock, which was ready and throbbing beneath his board shorts.

Ignoring his own need, he lifted his hand higher and cupped her breast over the material of her suit. Her nipple hardened, and he played with the distended tip with his fingers, his mouth still consuming hers.

She rocked her hips against his, the moans coming from deep in her throat, increasing his need.

He moved, gliding a hand from her breast downward, edging a finger beneath the elastic of her bathing suit, his fingertips slicking over her pussy, coating him in her arousal.

"You're so wet for me," he said, his voice gruff in her ear.

"Only for you. It's been so long."

At her words, he stilled, tipping his head back to meet her vulnerable gaze. "How long?" he asked.

"Over a year. I told you I have walls I don't let many people get past."

"Let's break them down," he said, trailing his finger over her wet folds until he found her clit and began a steady circular motion, pressing on the tight bud, building her desire. She rocked forward into his hand, and from her soft cries, he knew she was close.

He slid her bathing suit down her body, helping her to step out of it, leaving her completely bare to him. Which was a good thing because he intended to shatter all her walls and have her open to him completely.

He dropped to his knees, braced his hands on her thighs, and slid his tongue over her needy sex. She let out a startled cry. Her hands went to his hair, pulling on the strands as he began to lick and lap at her pussy, moving his tongue over and around her slick folds.

"Oh, Jake." Her thighs shook beneath his hands, and he took her higher with each lap of his tongue. She began to grind herself against his mouth, heedless of anything but the sensations rocking her body.

He wanted to give her more. He wanted to give her everything. Easing one hand between her thighs, he slid a finger inside her, curling his finger forward and finding the right spot to make her cry out in surprise.

Relentless, he pumped in and out while flicking his tongue over her clit. He sucked it into his mouth, grazed her with his teeth, then soothed her with loving laps of his tongue.

Suddenly she clenched around him, her inner walls grasping his finger, her entire body a shuddering bundle of need as she came hard. He slowed his ministrations, bringing her down slowly until her knees buckled and he caught her, lifting her into his arms.

"Good, baby?"

"The best," she murmured.

He grinned, carried her into the bedroom, and laid her down on his bed.

"Someone's overdressed," she said, eyeing his bathing suit shorts and tee shirt.

His gaze raked over her naked body in return, taking in milky white skin, full breasts, and neatly trimmed sex. God, she was spectacular.

He pulled his shirt off and tossed it to the floor. "Better?" he asked.

"Getting there," she said in a teasing tone.

He stripped off his shorts and kicked off his shoes, leaving him as bare as she was.

"Now that's what I wanted to see." Her hungry gaze raked over him. "Join me? I want to take advantage of whatever time we have."

"You say that like it's limited." If he had his way they were working toward something with a real future.

She shook her head. "I'm just saying we have to take the free time when we can."

"I'm all for that." He grabbed condoms from his nightstand drawer and tossed them onto the bed beside her.

✧　✧　✧

PHOEBE LAY NAKED on the bed, her heart beating hard inside her chest. She'd never felt more bared to anyone than she did to Jake in that moment. Her body had been sated, but one look at his gorgeous physique and she was revved up all over again.

She meant what she'd said, they needed to enjoy while they could. She didn't want to think too far into the future. Now was enough for her. The future was always uncertain.

Jake stood at the side of the bed, eyeing her like a treat he wanted to devour. One hand was on his cock, gliding his palm up and down before he climbed onto the bed and came down over her, his thick erection gliding over her damp sex.

"I waited years for this," he said, almost as if in awe.

She slid her fingers through his hair, gazing into his blue eyes. "Me, too."

His lips caught hers in a long, sweet kiss that quickly morphed into a hot, tongue-dueling one. He rolled his hips, the motion pressing his cock against her clit, waves of sensual pleasure traveling over her. With a moan, she arched upward, but he lifted himself off, depriving her of the friction of his body.

Instead he reached for the condom and tore it open with his teeth, then rolled it over his stiff erection. He knelt and brought his cock to her entrance. She was wet for him, and with one long thrust, he took her completely. She moaned, his silken thickness filling her until she felt every delectable inch of him.

A full-body shudder shook her, his fullness causing tremors of awareness to vibrate through her. She wanted friction. She wanted him to move. "Jake, I need you."

He groaned, gliding out slowly before sliding back in. "You have me."

A lump formed in her throat at his words, words that she'd needed to hear.

And then he began to move and she stopped thinking at all. His big body took command of hers, thrusting in and out, taking her higher every time they connected. She grabbed his shoulders, holding on as he picked up tempo and rhythm, taking her harder and higher with every drive home.

She gripped him tighter, nails scoring his back, her legs wrapping around his to hold him against her. She arched up, grinding herself into him, letting the waves take her over.

Her climax built, slowly at first, then a blinding burst of white stars sparkled behind her eyes, warmth and explosive sensations rocking her to her core.

A little while later, she lay curled in Jake's arms, flooded with gratitude for his return to her life. "I'm so glad you're here," she murmured.

"There's nowhere else I'd rather be than here with you."

She propped herself up on one arm. "I need to ask you something. And I'm not sure it's the right time, but I don't think there's ever a good time for this."

"Go for it. I have no secrets from you."

She drew a deep breath. "Why did you get divorced?" she asked.

He jerked as if surprised by the question. "That's complicated," he said eventually. "It ties to why I got married."

"Okay. I'm listening if you want to tell me." She laid her head on his chest, listening to his steady heartbeat, sensing it would be easier for him to tell her if he wasn't looking into her eyes.

He blew out a rough breath. "When I met Lindsay, I was at a low point in my life. I'd just gotten out of jail, but over time, things were looking good for me. Brent, her father, had taken me into his home and under his wing. She's a good woman and I wanted the kind of life we could have together."

"You haven't said you loved her," Phoebe said quietly.

He stroked the back of her hair with his hand. "I loved Lindsay. I'm just not sure I was ever *in* love with her."

Phoebe remained still and silent, processing his story and how it made her feel. A combination of sad for him and relieved for herself.

"Looking back, I was more in love with the idea of what we could be together. And the fact is, I hadn't gotten over you and Lindsay knew it."

"Jake." Phoebe sucked in a startled breath and pushed herself up to meet his gaze.

"It's always been you," he said, looking into her eyes. "It always will be."

Her heart squeezed tight at the admission, and she brushed her lips over his mouth. He slid his hand to the back of her neck and held her in place for a long, hard kiss. As selfish as it made her feel, she was glad he hadn't ever fallen deeply only to be hurt. That she'd had a hold on his heart, because he'd always held hers.

"So what's your relationship with Lindsay like now?" Phoebe asked when they finally parted.

He groaned. "That's complicated. Lindsay never got what she should have from me and eventually she became tired of looking for more. She asked for a divorce. It wasn't something I would have sought on my own. I'd have kept my family together, but when I realized I was making her unhappy, I agreed. Unfortunately, she was hoping to shock me into fighting for her. That didn't happen and she's been... hanging on to me in other ways ever since."

"What do you mean?"

"Well, the day I had to leave work because Callie had a stomach virus? She actually had a light stomachache and Lindsay basically sent me for a ginger ale run," he said with a frown. "It got me there, and when I realized the truth, I was pissed."

"You're a hard man to give up, Jake Nichols."

He treated her to a wry smile. "Look, would it be good if Callie could grow up with two parents who loved each other in one house? Yes, but that's not the way it's going to be."

He pulled Phoebe on top of him. "So now can we focus on us?"

"My pleasure." She kissed his lips, his chin, then steadily worked her way down, her lips following the light sprinkling of hair that led down to his groin.

He groaned, threading a hand in her hair as she licked, nipped, and made her way down to his straining erection. She grasped the thick shaft in her hand and slid her lips over the head, tasting the salty pre-come on the tip. She pulled off him, using suction that sounded like a pop, then licked the long stalk, palming his balls as she worked her way around him, tasting every last surface, coating him in damp warmth.

A phone rang in the background, but since it wasn't her ringtone and he didn't seem inclined to stop her, she continued her ministrations, pulling him deep into her mouth once more.

Wrapping a hand around the base, she glided her fingers up and down, sucking and swirling her tongue, twisting her grip around him at the same time.

He rocked his hips, thrusting upward into her mouth. She opened wider, accepting him deeper, and allowed him to slake his need inside her.

He pulled at her hair, groaning as he hit the back of her throat. Her eyes watered but she was determined to get him off this way, reveling in the power she had over his sexy body.

A few more swallows over him and he tugged on her hair. Ignoring the warning, she continued to suck until he came hard, spurting long streams of come into her mouth and down her throat.

She licked him clean, then crawled her way up his body, unable to hide the satisfied grin on her face. "Was it good for you?" she asked cheekily.

"Brat." He grinned and pulled her in for a kiss, obviously not caring that he could taste himself on her tongue.

The phone sounded again and he groaned. "That's mine," he muttered, sounding annoyed by the interruption. "I should check." He kissed her once more and climbed out of bed.

She couldn't tear her gaze from his fine body, taut ass, and well-muscled back.

"Lindsay," he bit off, answering the call. "Is Callie okay?"

Phoebe sat up in bed, pulling the covers over herself.

"Yeah. What was she doing on the damn thing? Never mind. I'll meet you there." He was reaching for his shorts before he ended the call.

"What's wrong?" she asked.

He glanced up and met her gaze. "Callie was on a swing set and fell off. Lindsay's afraid she broke her arm. They're on their way to the hospital."

JAKE DID HIS best to remain calm while inside he was in utter panic. His baby was so little. What if she'd done real damage? Was she in pain?

Phoebe jumped out of bed, not missing a beat. "I'll get dressed." She glanced around and ran out, obviously realizing her swimsuit was in the other room.

Jake met her in the entryway, car keys already in hand, to find her fully dressed and ready to go. As a mother, she understood the urgency of the situation. He didn't need to explain, and he was grateful for her calm presence.

"I can take a cab home or get an Uber," she said, reaching for her cell phone in her oversized bag.

"No." He shook his head, not wanting her to take herself home alone after what they'd shared. "Come with me. I'll get you home after."

She met his gaze, as if making sure he was certain,

then nodded. "Okay."

On the trip to the hospital, tension vibrated through him, worry for Callie the only thing on his mind. Phoebe placed her hand on his thigh and supported him silently, not saying a word. He pulled into the parking lot of the emergency room, and she ran out of the car, rushing to keep up with him as his long strides ate up the asphalt as they headed to the entrance.

He pushed through the heavy doors, and before he could process anything, Lindsay barreled into him, wrapping herself around him like she belonged in his arms.

Shit, he thought, suddenly aware of the thing he should have considered and would have if he hadn't been consumed with thoughts of his daughter in pain. Lindsay. Phoebe. Meeting for the first time. He was such an idiot.

Phoebe fell back as Lindsay, hysterically crying, remained latched on to Jake.

"What happened?" he asked his ex.

She sniffed into his tee shirt. "Mom's neighbor got a new swing set. She invited Callie over to play with her daughter. I was there, talking to the mom. Next thing I know, she's up too high and she lost her balance. She fell onto the ground, her arm at an odd angle. She was screaming, Jake."

He patted her back, trying to extricate himself as he spoke, shooting an uncomfortable Phoebe a remorseful glance. "Where is Callie now?" he asked, pulling at Lindsay's arms.

"Taking X-rays. They wouldn't let me come in with her." She sniffed and kept her head on his chest.

"Well, let's sit down and wait," he suggested, finally succeeding in peeling her off him.

Instead of taking the hint, she shoved her body beneath his arm, so he was holding her, as she turned and laid eyes on Phoebe, who waited in silence for the drama to end.

"Who are you?" Lindsay asked in a cool voice.

Jake managed to step away and regain his personal space. "Lindsay, this is Phoebe Gifford."

"Ward. Phoebe Ward. I took my aunt's last name when she brought me to live with her," Phoebe said quietly.

Funny how that hadn't had a chance to come up before now, Jake thought.

"Hello, Lindsay." Phoebe extended her hand politely.

Lindsay's gaze raked over Phoebe, taking in her swimsuit and cover up, cataloguing everything about her. "Phoebe. That's an unusual name," Lindsay said, ignoring Phoebe's outstretched hand until Phoebe finally dropped her arm to her side. "It can't be… You can't be that Phoebe…" Lindsay trailed off.

Jake did his best not to wince at her rudeness… and the fact that with the utterance of Phoebe's name, everything obviously clicked in Lindsay's mind.

When they'd first met, he'd told her everything about his long-lost love, before they'd gotten together as a couple. And she'd held it over his head throughout their marriage, the fact that he couldn't give enough of himself to her because he'd never gotten over Phoebe.

"Jake?" Lindsay's voice took on an edge of panic as she looked up at him, silently begging him to deny the obvious.

"Relax," Jake said, his voice the epitome of a calm he didn't feel, kicking himself for causing this scene. "This isn't the time or the place. I wanted to tell you, but you canceled my weekend with Callie so I wasn't going to see you. But I planned to discuss… things… with you."

Clearly now wasn't the time to mention his son.

"How could you bring her here?" Lindsay asked, her hysteria still clear.

"I should go," Phoebe said, gathering her bag closer to her but straightening her shoulders, refusing to get in the middle of a situation she hadn't created.

"Yes, go. You don't belong here," Lindsay stated.

"No. Stay. You're with me." Jake knew the words

would hurt his ex-wife, but there was no way to help it. "Lindsay, Phoebe and I were together when you called about Callie. I didn't want to take the time to drive her home before coming to see about my girl."

"*Our* girl," Lindsay reminded him. "Yours and mine. Not—"

"I'm looking for Callie Nichols' parents?" A doctor had stepped into the room and called out, looking around.

"Here," Jake said.

"I'm her mother." Lindsay rushed over to the man.

The older man had a chart in his hand as he faced them. "She has a fracture in her forearm. The good news is the growth plate wasn't impacted. We're going to put her in a cast for three to four weeks. I suggest you follow up with a pediatric orthopedist on Monday. In the meantime, you can be there when we do the cast, if you'll come with me."

Jake nodded. He turned to Phoebe, who gestured for him to go with the doctor, and Lindsay, who was pulling on his hand, urging him to go with her immediately.

He wished he had time to go to her, to make sure she was okay after the scene with Lindsay, but the hard truth was, his daughter needed him now. Phoebe was a mom and she'd understand where his priorities had to be. But that didn't stop him from looking back over his shoulder to see her pulling her phone out of her bag.

"Phoebe, wait for me," he called out.

She waved at him, gesturing for him to go, and having no choice, he rushed to see his daughter.

PHOEBE WAITED UNTIL Jake walked through the swinging doors and into the emergency room proper before dialing her sister's number. "Hey, Halley. I need a ride home from the hospital and don't panic. I'm fine." She went on to explain the situation, then settled in to wait for her sister to come pick her up.

Her day had been a roller coaster, starting with the nerves of being with Jake and Jamie in a family-like situation. Although it had been short, Jamie had relaxed around Jake, and for a second get-together as father and son, it had gone well. Jake had even mentioned going out alone with Jamie, and if her son was ready, it was okay with Phoebe. She trusted Jake.

And maybe that was why she'd been ready to go home with him. Because they connected on a soul-deep level and she had that trust for him she hadn't had with any other man. Even the few guys she'd allowed herself to sleep with, it'd been more with the hope of getting closer to them and never reaching that point, even after being intimate with them. Whereas with Jake, she'd felt that closeness even prior to having sex. Sex had just cemented what she'd known since she was a young girl. Jake was special.

With Jake, she'd let go and felt carefree… until they'd reached the hospital. Before she could let her mind go to the scene with Lindsay, her sister pulled up in her red SUV.

Only once she was safely inside the vehicle did she text Jake and let him know she'd gotten a ride and he should focus on taking care of his daughter. She'd asked him to let her know how Callie was doing once he'd gotten her home and settled.

"Talk to me, Phoebe," Halley said as she pulled out of the hospital parking lot. "You told me briefly on the phone that you met his ex. What happened?"

She gave her sister the rundown. "But I'm fine. I just didn't think it was my place to stick around and pull Jake in two different directions. I'm a grown-up. I can take care of myself. He needs to be with his little girl."

"And the witchy ex?"

Phoebe managed a laugh. "An apt description."

"Hey, you told me how she clung to Jake and wouldn't even shake your hand. That tells me all I need to know." She frowned as she drove, her focus on the road.

"Honestly, Jake said she wants him back—on her

terms—and he claims it's not going to happen. But she's not above using her child as leverage." Although Phoebe had understood the other woman's panic over her daughter's fall, her drama hadn't been about Callie. It had been centered on Jake, and that had been before she'd caught sight of Phoebe. And it had shaken her up, to see how much the other woman not only wanted him but how badly she'd act to get and keep his attention.

Phoebe believed Jake when he said he was over her, but they had a child together, they'd already lived together as a family, and who was to say she wouldn't lure him back in?

Phoebe had a lot of life experience when it came to being left alone. First her mother, the one person who was supposed to love and protect her, had abandoned her to the state. Then, the foster family she'd trusted and liked had turned Jake out, showing her how easy it would be to disappoint them and have them drop her next.

And then she'd lost Jake, which had ripped her heart to shreds. Was it any wonder she hadn't let any other man in? She was a textbook case of a woman in fear of being hurt and abandoned, not that she'd given it any thought before now. But she'd never been faced with being able to proactively protect herself before. She could now.

"Obviously Lindsay has issues," Halley said. "It's sad that she wasn't happy in her marriage, and it's even sadder that she's still trying to hold on to Jake now that it's over. And that was her choice, from what you told me."

"Well, that's because she wants him to love her the way she deserves. He said she didn't get that from him, and maybe I should feel bad... but I mostly feel sorry for her because she can't let go." And her stomach twisted with the knowledge that the woman would constantly be pulling at Jake and making demands. She didn't think she could handle living with what she perceived to be uncertainty.

"Do you worry Jake won't be able to extricate himself from her? And can you handle the drama that comes along with him?" Halley asked, astutely echoing Phoebe's concerns.

She bit down on her bottom lip. "Yeah, I worry he'll feel compelled to choose her somewhere down the road. And no, I couldn't handle that."

"Oh, Phoebe," Halley said as they arrived at the main house, pulling past the circular drive.

Phoebe shook her head, not wanting her sister's pity. "I also have Jamie to worry about, and Jake hasn't told Lindsay about him yet. You can imagine how that's going to go over." And she refused to let her son be subjected to Lindsay, her moods or her jealousy.

Halley blew out a long breath. "Okay, that's fair but it's not everything. You can work that out. Don't use him as an excuse to pull away. Don't you remember all my fears? And how you insisted I put the past behind me?"

Phoebe treated Halley to a wry smile. "And you didn't find it easy, did you?" Her sister hadn't moved forward until she'd been good and ready.

"Unfair, using my own weaknesses against me," Halley said, laughing.

Phoebe chuckled at that. "We certainly were given reason to have fear of commitment."

Halley nodded. "We were. But if I can figure out this love thing, you can, too. And deep down, you know what you want."

But what Phoebe wanted and what she could handle—or was willing to risk—were two very different things.

Chapter Seven

"BYE, MUNCHKIN." JAKE kissed his sleeping daughter's cheek and walked out of her room. The day had been endless, from Callie's crying during the setting of the cast to settling her in Lindsay's car for the ride home to the drugstore run for painkillers to the viewing of *Beauty and the Beast* to distract Callie from the pain. Jake had been solely focused on his daughter.

Still, when he'd gotten Phoebe's text that she left with her sister and he should concentrate on Callie, his stomach had twisted in a painful knot. Leaving Phoebe alone after making love to her all day hadn't been in his plan. And to do it after Lindsay's clingy irrational behavior hadn't helped. Even if he should have handled the whole situation better or at least thought ahead. Now he had the fun job of telling his ex-wife he had a son with his first love.

He stepped out of Callie's room to find Lindsay

waiting for him in the hallway. Since going in to see Callie in the hospital, she hadn't brought up Phoebe, and he knew that was about to change. He might as well be proactive about it.

"Lindsay, can we talk?" he asked, following her down the hall to the kitchen.

She narrowed her brown eyes at him. "I'm not sure we have anything to say."

So she was playing the wounded party. "Lindsay, look, I wanted to talk to you before you found out about Phoebe. We ran into each other again on one of my jobs and we… reconnected."

She picked up a dishtowel and began wiping down the clean counter. "I'll just bet you did—reconnect," she said, wrinkling her nose in disgust.

He held on to his temper. "I'm sorry you're upset, but we aren't married anymore."

She tossed the towel onto the counter and turned, folding her arms across her chest. "And why is that?" she asked. "Because she was always between us."

"Not intentionally, you know that. I tried my best to be a good husband." Lindsay had just been too perceptive, noticing that he'd held back a part of his heart. He hadn't meant to be distant. Just like she hadn't meant to be overly needy. Or maybe he'd caused that behavior in her. Who knew.

He shook his head. "There's no point in rehashing

this subject. I ran into Phoebe again and we're involved now, but there's something else you need to know."

"What's that?"

He drew a deep breath. "When she was sixteen, she gave birth to my son."

A half hour of dramatic crying later, Jake walked out of his ex-wife's house, drained and exhausted. He'd made it clear to Lindsay that he intended to be a parent to Jamie and that meant Callie would be meeting her brother. She'd sobbed about how she'd wanted a big family with him, that they should all be together. And that she'd only asked for the divorce to shake him up and make him see what they'd be losing. She'd rehashed it all until his head hurt.

He settled into his truck and pulled out his cell. He'd checked in with Phoebe once, letting her know Callie was on her way home and he'd be tied up for the afternoon.

And he called her again now but she didn't answer, so despite being weary, he drove over to her house and knocked on her front door.

She answered, wearing a short floral robe. Her hair was pulled up in a high bun, and her cheeks were flushed, strands of hair that fell around her face damp. Even with no makeup, she was still beautiful. She'd obviously just gotten out of the shower, and despite the late hour and his exhaustion, his body responded to seeing her, his cock stiffening in his pants.

"Jake!" she said, obviously surprised. "Come on in." She tightened the sash on her robe, which only served to expose her cleavage. He swallowed hard, knowing he couldn't walk in and jump her without conversation first.

She stepped aside to let him in. "How is Callie?"

He thought of his baby lying in her bed with a bright pink cast on her arm. "Uncomfortable. Sleeping off the codeine. But at least that means she's not feeling pain anymore," he said.

Her expression softened. "I'm sorry. It hurts when your baby is in pain." She gave him an understanding smile. "Umm, can I get you anything to eat or drink?"

He was starving… for more than food, given how delicious she looked, but she wasn't giving him signals that she felt the same way. And he hadn't come here for her to take care of him.

"No, thanks. I just came by to make sure you're okay. I know today was rough." That meeting in the hospital couldn't have gone worse.

"I'm fine." She placed a hand on his arm, then obviously thought better and quickly removed it. Whatever barriers he'd torn down earlier today, she'd put back up even higher now. "I take it Lindsay was upset about seeing me."

"Yeah. And more upset about Jamie. I told her. He's at his friend Matthew's, right?" he asked.

She shook her head. "Actually he ended up coming home after dinner. But he's asleep." She lowered her voice just in case. "I'm sorry Lindsay is upset but that can't be my concern. My son's welfare comes first in this… mess."

"I know, I get it and I agree."

"Are you sure?" She straightened her shoulders, the protective mom coming to the surface. "Because the woman I met is unpredictable. I know eventually you're going to want to be with Jamie alone, without me. If Lindsay is going to see him or meet him when she brings Callie to you, if she's liable to be anything but kind, I won't allow him to be exposed to her. You have to understand that."

He admired her fierce defense of her child, and he felt exactly the same way because Jamie was his son, too. He already loved the boy and he'd do anything to protect him. "You can be sure I'll make it clear to Lindsay about all of it."

Phoebe inclined her head. "Good. I'm glad we got this sorted out." She started to lead him back to the front door, as if they had nothing left to discuss.

As if she hadn't spent the earlier part of the day in his bed.

But she had, and he wasn't about to let her run

from everything they'd shared. "Phoebe, are you upset with me about Lindsay and what happened today?"

She turned back to him and shook her head. "You can't control her behavior."

"But?" Because something was wrong.

She blew out a long breath. "But today was proof of the fact that things are complicated between us. Maybe too complicated."

"Do you really think I'm about to let external factors get between us?" he asked.

"You might not have a choice. Sometimes it's not about what we want. Not when you're a parent. It might not be the right time for us." He felt like she was saying it might never be the right time.

And when she looked at him sadly, his stomach twisted with real fear that he couldn't get through to her.

Time to retreat and regroup, he thought, because now that he'd found her again, he wasn't willing to let her go.

MIDWEEK, PHOEBE SAT at her desk in the office, trying to work but preoccupied by her personal life. Tonight Jamie was going for dinner with Jake— without her. He planned to tell Jamie that he had a sister, and though he'd invited Phoebe to come, she'd insisted father and son get to know one another without her as a buffer. And she'd meant it.

She'd also used it as an excuse not to be around Jake.

Because when she was around him, she wanted him. And this weekend had not only shown her how difficult their lives would be if they were together, it had raised her childhood fears and insecurities.

As for Jamie, Phoebe's pulling away from Jake would protect him. An insecure woman like Jake's ex was bound to take her jealousy out on Phoebe's son, but if Phoebe took herself out of the equation, Lindsay would mellow out and be forced to accept Jake as a part of his and Callie's life.

She was doing what was best for her son. And retreating due to self-preservation.

Her desk phone rang and she answered, seeing it was the receptionist at the front desk. "Hi, Claudia."

"Hi, Phoebe. There's someone here who wants to buy a house. He's asked for you."

She frowned, knowing she usually booked in advance and walk-ins were rare, but she didn't have any appointments this afternoon, so she had time. "Send him back, please."

She stacked the papers she'd been working on and waited for her new client.

"Hi there," a familiar masculine voice said.

Her stomach flipped over as she looked up into blue eyes she knew well. "Jake, what in the world are you doing here?"

He slid into the chair across from her desk, looking sexy in a light blue tee shirt that accentuated his eyes, and folded his arms across his muscular chest.

"I'm at a real estate office because I need a house. My apartment is too small for my newly expanded family," he explained, a pleased grin on his face because he'd obviously found a way to spend time with her that she couldn't object to.

She had to admit she admired his creativity, she thought wryly. "Well, welcome to Walsh Real Estate. What kind of house are you interested in?"

"I'm looking for three bedrooms. A small fourth for an office wouldn't hurt."

"A bedroom for each child," she murmured, writing down his qualifications, impressed he was working his future home around both children.

"It doesn't seem fair to make them share one. A boy and a girl, and they need time to get to know each other without being forced down each other's throats. On top of that, I'm ready for more space."

"Are you looking in Rosewood Bay, which is my area of expertise or did you want to stay in Thornton, in which case I can still help you out, I'll just need to do more research?" she said in her most professional voice.

"I'll look in both towns and any other nearby areas you might recommend."

"Good. I'll need some time to pull listings. If you'd like, we can schedule an appointment to go looking or I can call you once I'm ready."

"No. Let's schedule now. I know how busy you can get. I wouldn't want you not to have time for me."

She didn't miss the point behind that statement. She had been avoiding him. She blushed, feeling the heat rush across her cheeks. "Okay, then." This weekend was the Fourth of July and she had plans for a picnic with Jamie and his friend's parents on Saturday. Sunday evening was the fireworks in town.

"How's Tuesday after the holiday weekend?"

"That works for me. I don't have anyone scheduled at the Renault place that I have to oversee."

She nodded. "Good." She added his name to the calendar on her smartphone and met his gaze. "So we have a plan."

"We do."

He rose to his feet just as Harvey stepped around the corner and caught sight of Phoebe with a client. She knew the drill. He claimed to enjoy meeting clients, but the fact was, he liked to puff out his chest and be introduced as the owner of the company.

She stood and forced a smile. "Harvey, you're just

time to meet Jake Nichols. Jake, this is Harvey ~~lsh~~, the owner of Walsh Real Estate."

"Good to meet you, Jake. I'm assuming my girl Phoebe is taking good care of you," he said as he extended his hand in greeting.

Jake stiffened at his use of the term *my girl*, and Phoebe shot him a pleading look not to cause trouble.

Jake shook Harvey's hand with what Phoebe assumed was too firm a grip based on how her boss winced. But his ego prevented him from saying a word.

"Buying or selling?" Harvey asked Jake.

"Buying."

"Well, good luck. I know Phoebe will help you find exactly what you're looking for." He turned and walked away, leaving Jake glaring after him.

"So that's the prick?"

"Jake!" she hissed. "That's my boss and this is my place of business."

"Fine. But I don't have to like how he treats you. He's disrespectful and he's a pig. I want you out of here."

"Well, you don't get a vote. This is how I make my living. Now will you please calm down?"

Closing his eyes, he inhaled a couple of deep breaths before facing her again. "I'm sorry. I don't mean to make this harder for you."

She nodded. "I know he's hard to take. So…" She decided a subject change was in order. "What time are you picking up Jamie tonight?"

"How's six?" he asked.

"He'll be ready."

He braced one arm on her desk, leaning in closer. "Are you sure I can't convince you to join us?" His sexy cologne teased her senses, both the man and his request so very tempting.

But she'd promised herself she would maintain her distance and protect herself from future heartache. *Be smart now, don't get overly invested, then you won't get hurt later*, she reminded herself.

"I'm going to enjoy my much-needed night by myself," she said. "A hot bath, a good book, a glass of wine. Bliss."

She smiled, knowing deep down it was forced, because she'd much rather spend her evening with Jake and Jamie than alone and lonely in her claw-foot bathtub.

THE FOURTH OF July evening arrived, providing a clear and cloudless sky for the fireworks to come. Every year since Phoebe moved to Rosewood Bay, she'd gone to the fireworks show put on by the town. Her aunt had taken them when they were teenagers, hoping to introduce them to local traditions and friends. While Phoebe made friends easily, she hadn't kept them all after they'd discovered she was pregnant. There were parents who hadn't wanted their daughters around a *bad influence*. But there were friends who had stood by her, and she had those friendships through today.

"Jamie, are you almost ready to go?" she called out to her son.

"Coming!"

But of course he didn't materialize immediately. He was probably still on his X-Box finishing a game. He was so easygoing and resilient, she thought. He'd adapted so quickly to having a father in his life, and he'd come home from his last outing with Jake excited to inform her he had a half sister and a grandma he couldn't wait to meet.

Her heart gave a small twist at the notion of him having another family that had nothing to do with her, but that was life. As long as he was happy and thriving, she could cope with things as they were.

She glanced at the time on her phone. "Jamie!" she called again.

"I'm here!" He skidded to a halt in front of her, wearing his favorite pair of cargo shorts and a tee shirt. "Matthew's going to be at the fireworks and he's bringing his dog. Cameron said he'll be there, too. Can we go now?"

She shook her head, amused, because hadn't she been calling him to come for the last five minutes? "I'm ready. I threw the picnic blanket in the trunk so we have something to sit on."

They climbed into the car and headed to the park, which was adjacent to a private country club. The town partnered with the club so they could have the right vantage point from which to provide the night's entertainment.

They arrived and found a parking spot, which wasn't easy given how crowded the area already was, and she looked for Halley and Kane, who'd said they would meet her there. While looking for her family, Phoebe talked to people she'd known for years, friends she agreed to meet up with for lunch, and clients for whom she'd bought and sold homes.

"There they are!" Jamie pointed toward a prime spot that her sister had snagged, and Phoebe headed in that direction. Jamie had already run to greet his aunt, Kane, and their dog, Monty, a black bundle of fur who was sitting beside them, wagging his tail.

"Good job, you two," Phoebe said as she dumped her blanket and bag onto the ground.

"Thank Aunt Joy. She was the ultra-early one. She went off to talk to one of her friends." Halley patted her hand on her blanket on the ground, indicating ebe should sit.

amie was already petting Monty and talking to the dog.

"Jamie, I see Matthew with his parents. Do you want to invite him to sit with us?" Phoebe asked as she settled in cross-legged on the blanket.

He shook his head. "They have Rover. Can I sit with them instead? Please?"

New puppy or dog he was used to. Of course he wanted the shiny new puppy. "Go ahead," she agreed.

Kane, who sat with one arm around Halley, laughed. "I'm thinking the boy needs his own dog."

"Bite your tongue," Phoebe said good-naturedly. "I have enough to do on a daily basis without taking care of another living being. And the good news is, he hasn't asked for a pet."

"Yet," Halley said, leaning into Kane.

"Hi, everyone." Aunt Joy strode over and joined them, a tentative smile on her face when she glanced at Phoebe.

They hadn't been together face-to-face since Phoebe had found out her aunt had lied about not finding Jake.

"Hi, Aunt Joy." Phoebe stood and hugged her aunt, breaking the ice.

After all, she had a child who she'd do anything to keep safe. She understood that her aunt's heart had been in the right place, even if she didn't like the result.

"Hi, honey." She hugged her, too, before pulling back, a look of understanding passing between them. There was no need to rehash things. "Where's my nephew?" she asked.

"Over with his friend." She pointed to where Jamie was wrestling on the ground with the dog and his friend Matthew.

Aunt Joy shook her head, an indulgent smile on her face. "Boys will be boys."

"That they will."

They both sat down on the blanket again, Phoebe tucking her legs beneath her. Ever since they'd arrived, it had been getting progressively darker. The fireworks wouldn't start until it was nightfall, and so they waited, enjoying each other's company and relaxing.

Phoebe leaned back on her hands, looking around, catching sight of a man who looked just like Jake. Because she had Jake on her mind, that's why, she thought.

For the last however many years, she hadn't run into him anywhere. There was no way he'd be at a Rosewood Bay town event. Except when he came closer and she looked twice, it really *was* Jake. Her stomach flipped and she let out a gasp.

"What's wrong?" Halley asked.

"Jake's here," she whispered to her sister. "Jet-black hair, jeans, and a white tee shirt. Walking this way."

"He's hot," she murmured. "I'd whistle but my guy over here might get upset." Halley laughed and Kane pulled her into a hug.

"Damn right I'd get upset." He brushed a kiss over her cheek.

Phoebe rolled her eyes at the couple, but her concentration was on Jake, who was clearly looking around for someone… and then his gaze zeroed in on her.

A wide grin covered his face. "Phoebe."

"Jake." She pushed herself to her feet. "What are you doing here?" She tried not to wince at how rude she sounded, but she really was surprised.

"Jamie told me about the fireworks display. He said I should come see it. So here I am."

Oh my God. She was going to kill her son. Not really. It was sweet that he wanted his father here, but it would have been nice if he'd mentioned the fact that he'd informed Jake of their plans. She could have at least mentally prepared herself for—

"Hi, I'm Halley, Phoebe's sister." She and Kane had stood to meet him. "I've heard so much about you," her sister said, beginning the family introductions it would have been nice to have had a chance to brace herself for.

Jake smiled. "Jake Nichols and nice to meet you. I've heard a lot about you, too. All good, of course."

She laughed. "And this is my boyfriend, Kane Harmon."

"Kane," Jake said.

The two men shook hands, no appraising each other or testosterone-infused issues.

"Jamie tells me you've been great, helping him with baseball," Jake said to Kane. He hesitated, then said, "Thank you. I'm glad he's had you in his life when I couldn't be there."

Phoebe's heart squeezed in her chest for all Jake had missed in Jamie's young life.

Kane waved away the comment. "He's a great kid. It's been my pleasure."

Aunt Joy came up to them then, her expression uncertain. "Phoebe? I'd like to meet Jamie's father."

Phoebe swallowed hard, then stepped next to Jake to show her aunt that no matter what he'd done in the past, she sided with him now, as her son's dad. "Aunt Joy, this is Jake Nichols, Jamie's father." She drew a deep breath. "Jake, this is my aunt. Joy Ward."

He studied her for a silent moment, probably thinking about how it was her fault he hadn't known about his son for all these years.

Phoebe braced herself in case he decided to express himself on the subject, but Jake merely extended his hand. "It's nice to meet you," he finally said, taking Phoebe by surprise.

Aunt Joy shook his hand. "Yes. I... look forward to getting to know you better."

Before things could get more awkward, a loud bang sounded, followed by flashes of colored light in the sky.

Halley and Kane settled into each other's arms on their blanket to watch the show, and Aunt Joy sat down beside them, leaving Phoebe standing with Jake.

"So where is Jamie?" he asked.

"He found the same friend with the puppy and decided to sit with their family for the fireworks."

Jake laughed. "It's got to be the lure of the dog. Okay, so do you want to sit down and watch the show?" He gestured to the empty spots on the over-sized blanket.

She drew a deep breath and nodded, nervous about being with him again since she'd drawn those mental lines around what could be between them.

But he was here and she couldn't be rude. "Sure. Let's sit."

She eased down onto the ground, and he sat beside her, his big body touching hers. Together they looked up at the sparkling stars and other explosions of color in the sky, taking in the beauty in silence but for the pops, bangs, and loud crackling noises above them.

The show was spectacular, made more so by the fact that she sat beside Jake in comfortable silence. For how many years had she come to this very place and dreamed of him, wondered where he was, how he was doing? Losing him had gutted her, and getting over him had been a long, slow process. Over time, she'd stopped thinking and yearning... except for some lonely nights when she would lie in bed and long for him and his strong arms around her.

She understood now they'd been little more than children, but the feelings, those had been very real.

Without warning, his hand came to cover hers, warm, solid, and steady.

"It's beautiful," she said, not pulling back from his touch, her gaze on the sky.

Just a few minutes, she told herself. She'd enjoy the moment.

"It is."

He sounded so close, she turned to find him watching her and not the night sky. "Beautiful," he echoed in a whisper.

The way he looked at her, as if she was as stunning as the cascading flares in the darkness, made her breath catch in her throat.

They were surrounded by people, but as intently as he studied her, they might as well be alone. And if he leaned closer, his lips would be on hers and the explosions around them would be happening inside her body. But he merely squeezed her hand tighter and they continued to watch the display above.

It was a tender, sweet moment that warmed her heart and made her wish for things she was desperately afraid of having… and losing again.

THE FIELD WHERE everyone had spread out to watch the fireworks slowly emptied, everyone walking back to their cars. Some held rolled-up blankets, others folding chairs as they made their way. Knowing he probably wasn't parked anywhere near Phoebe, Jake nevertheless walked her and Jamie back to their vehicle.

After Jamie had told him about their annual family fireworks outing, he'd innocently invited him to join them. Jake had debated, knowing Phoebe probably wouldn't want him there and deciding that was as good a reason as any to go—to push past the barrier she'd erected between them. Nothing would happen if he couldn't show her how good they could be together, and to do that, they had to be… well, together.

Even her aunt's presence hadn't ruined his mood or deterred him from his plan to make her want more. Not that he was comfortable around the woman.

She'd judged him and found him lacking as a teenager. He doubted she thought he was good enough for her niece, but to her credit, she'd asked to meet him and had shaken his hand.

For Phoebe's sake, he'd resolved to put the past behind him. He didn't fault her completely for the choice she'd made. He owned his role in ending up in prison.

"Rover's not housebroken," Jamie said, interrupting Jake's thoughts. "He shits everywhere."

"Language, mister," Phoebe automatically said.

"Sorry. That's what Matthew's dad said. He's mad."

Jake understood his frustration. "Dog training takes patience. It's not for the weak," he said, laughing.

"Mom, can we get a puppy?" Jamie asked. "I'll do all the work. I'll walk him and feed him and train him, I promise."

Jake wasn't surprised by the question. It had only been a matter of time before Jamie asked. Make that begged. He didn't know what Phoebe would say, but he was certain that as soon as the novelty of the puppy wore off for Jamie, all the work would be hers. He didn't envy her dealing with this.

"I'm sorry, honey. It's just not possible," she said, regret in her tone. "I work full time, you're in school, and the dog would be alone too often. It wouldn't be fair to the puppy."

Jamie mumbled something under his breath and his legs dragged as they continued their walk to the car.

Jake felt bad for both of them. "At least your Aunt Halley has a dog you can see anytime you want," he said, trying to cheer Jamie up.

The boy didn't reply.

They reached Phoebe's car and she popped the trunk. Jake put the blanket, which he'd insisted on carrying, inside and closed it again.

"This was fun," he said, glancing at Jamie, who was still sulking and still looking down at the ground in full-on grump mode.

"It *was* nice." Phoebe met his gaze.

"Special," he said for her ears alone, thinking of the moment when he'd looked over and caught her watching the show in awe, her delicate profile tipped toward the sky.

He'd drunk her in, well aware of how perfect that moment was, how fortunate they were to have had it given how they'd been separated once before.

"Jamie, say good-bye to your dad," Phoebe said.

Jake turned, too often still caught off guard and humbled that this boy was his son.

"Bye, Dad," Jamie said and stomped his way around the car, letting himself inside.

Jake stared after him, dumbfounded. "Did he just call me—"

"Yeah," Phoebe said, breathless and sounding as shocked as he felt. "He hasn't done that before? Like when you were alone this past week?"

Jake shook his head, his heart beating hard and in his throat. From the stunned look on Phoebe's face, she knew exactly what this moment meant to him.

And there was nobody he'd rather share it with.

Chapter Eight

P HOEBE NEVER SHOULD have agreed to let Jake pick her up for their day of house viewings. She should have taken her own car. Instead she'd found herself saying yes, he could swing by at nine a.m. And since she'd printed all the listings last night, she didn't need to go to the office, and he pulled up to her house on time.

She climbed into his truck, only too aware of his enticing masculine scent in the small confines of the front cab and how delicious he looked in a pair of jeans, a faded gray tee shirt, and his sexy sunglasses on his eyes.

She'd chosen her normal cream-colored suit for the showings, wanting to be her professional self. She smiled at him. "Good morning. Ready to go see some houses?"

He nodded but he didn't tear his gaze from hers, leaving no doubt that although she'd put on her professional armor, he liked what he saw.

"So how was the rest of your weekend?" he asked.

"Good. I slept in yesterday, and by the time I woke up, Jamie had stopped sulking over the fact that I said no to getting a dog. I called that a win and it was a good day."

He laughed, one arm on the top of the steering wheel. "I hear you. Callie and I spent the day at our town pool, even though she can't get the cast wet, then I took her for pizza and brought her back to her mom's."

"Sounds fun."

"It was. Speaking of Callie, I wanted to get her and Jamie together next weekend. Is he free?"

She knew his schedule by heart. "He has a baseball game on Saturday afternoon at two. He's free after and on Sunday."

He paused in thought, then asked, "Would it be okay if I brought Callie to the game? It might be a good icebreaker if he's in his element. At Callie's age, she'll be happy just being with me for the day and doing something different."

Phoebe thought about it and nodded. "That should be fine. I think he'd like you to come see him. And I know he can't wait to meet Callie."

"Good. We can go for dinner after," he suggested, putting the car in drive.

Oh no. Going out as a family? That was a dangerous thing for her too eager heart. "Don't you think
you should take your children out together?" she
asked, meaning alone together, just the three of them,
without her added to the mix.

He rolled his shoulders in an easy shrug. "That's
what I'll be doing. You'll just be joining us," he said,
obviously not wanting to take no for an answer.

And she really didn't have a good reason to push
the issue and refuse… so she remained silent.

Her worry about getting too immersed in his life
was her own concern. He wasn't aware of her fear that
she'd get too invested and then he'd leave her for his
ex or some other reason in the future. And she wasn't
about to explain it to him now.

"So where's the first house?" he asked, changing
the subject.

Relieved, she gave him directions as he drove, and
they pulled up to a small center-hall Colonial. "So this
one was built in 1965, but it has had a lot of renova-
tion done in the last few years. The kitchen and the
bathrooms are remodeled and the roof is new, which
is always a good thing."

She had a key, and the family, knowing she was
bringing a potential buyer, had made themselves
scarce. She found the family being gone helpful so her
client could feel free to say anything they wanted in the

course of the showing. Of course, sometimes the seller was home and her buyer spoke their mind anyway, which was always an awkward situation and was why she encouraged the sellers to go out during a visit.

"I suppose new is good," he said. "Although considering the business I'm in, I don't mind doing work to get the place into the shape." He parked at the curb and glanced up at the house.

From the street, it gave an impressive first glance. The shrubbery had been well maintained and the driveway recently sealed. She wasn't sure why this family was looking to move, but they'd be turning over a beautiful house when they sold.

They walked through rather quickly. "The bedrooms are upstairs," she said as they climbed the stairs.

The minute he walked into the master bedroom, he shook his head. "Way too small. I'd be claustrophobic in here," he said with a full-on shudder.

She encouraged him to look at the rest of the house anyway, but soon they were back in the car.

He blew out a breath. "Next?" he said, laughing.

She smiled and sorted through her papers. Based on his reaction to this place, she chose one that was the complete opposite.

She directed him to their next home, on the other side of Rosewood Bay. "Now this one was built in the late 1970s, and it has been updated, just not recently, so it's dated and will show age. I'd tell most people they have to have vision for this house, but I think you already know that. And of course, the price reflects the lack of added value over the years."

"Let's see," he said, excited, clearly not discouraged by the datedness of the property.

They walked into the home with white-painted shingles on the outside and black shutters on the windows. Inside, the hardwood floors were in good condition, as she pointed out to him, and he walked into the large kitchen, smiling at what he saw.

"These old cabinets are easy enough to replace, but look at the size of this room." A large round table sat in the corner with five chairs around it. At a glance, it was a lot bigger than the last home.

"I can see us in here," he said and her body jolted at the word *us*.

He had to have meant him and the kids, so she didn't call him out on it, because she could see herself here, too, sipping coffee in the morning while looking out at the wooded landscape.

Drawing a deep breath, she led the way through to the family room, which had a fireplace and a full wall for a television unit, then passed through a small formal dining room.

"So no stairs, which some people find a plus," she said as they headed to the back of the house since it was a one-story structure.

"Here are the kids' rooms," she said, stepping aside so he could enter the first one. Although small, it wasn't too tiny. There was a dresser and twin bed, but plenty of floor space, and should he want a double bed, he could go that route. The same for the next bedroom.

"And here's the master," she said. "The beauty of this is that it's been added on to over the years." The far wall had a row of windows overlooking the wooded area, which was beautiful, especially in the summertime, which it now was. "So it's fairly large. And it has an office attached."

He walked through, studying the room in silence. She waited, giving him time to take it all in.

"This layout is perfect," he said at last. "And because it's a one-story, there's easy potential for adding on over the years."

She nodded. Only someone with money to renovate or vision and ability would fall in love with this older home. It needed some TLC, which she knew he could provide.

"I like it," he said, sounding excited. "Can I see the backyard? I want there to be room for a swing set and a place for the kids to play."

She smiled. "Of course." She led him out back, which he fell in love with, again for its potential. There was a patio, which had seen better days but had room to expand and make it larger, and an empty grass space before the woods for the play structure he wanted, and he was grinning as they walked back to the truck.

"Let's see what else you've got but keep this one in mind."

They spent the next few hours seeing a total of four more homes, none which suited him better than the ranch.

She discovered that when he was ready, Jake could be impulsive. He told her to make an offer at a number he named below list value because of the renovations needed.

Since she had paperwork to do for him, she expected him to head toward her office or her house so she could get her car, but he drove in the opposite direction instead.

"Where are we going?" she asked.

"It's lunchtime and I don't know about you but I'm starving. Do you still like Chinese?"

"Yes, but—"

"But you have plans? Somewhere you need to be? I was under the impression you'd blocked the day off for me. I know you had more houses to show me if I'd wanted to go."

She pursed her lips. "Yes, but you didn't."

"So let's eat."

Her traitorous stomach chose that moment to growl in a very unladylike manner.

"And I'll take that as a yes," he said, laughing.

He stopped at a takeout place on the way to his apartment, because, he said, it was the best Chinese food around. She let him choose for them and soon they were back in his apartment. She couldn't forget the last time they were alone here, what had happened between them, and how much she wanted a repeat performance despite common sense telling her otherwise.

Instead of sitting at the small kitchen table, he loaded up the boxes on the table in the family room, set chopsticks that came with inside each box, and told her to dig in.

"Remember when we learned to use these together?" She laughed, recalling the night the Dawsons had brought home cartons just like these and handed out the chopsticks. "I ended up wearing more than I ate."

He grinned. "You weren't all that nimble with them, that's for sure."

She blushed at the memory. "You took my hands in yours and hand-fed me until I figured it out."

"I'm shocked Mrs. Dawson didn't figure out what was going on between us then."

She paused, the lo mein halfway to her mouth, surprised he'd brought up that part of their past.

Maybe he really had made peace with everything. If so, he'd found it easier than she had.

She finished her bite, then met his gaze. "I'm—"

"Do not say you're sorry. It's over and I don't regret anything we did together."

"Me, neither," she admitted.

While they finished their Chinese food, which was, as he'd promised, among the best she'd ever eaten, they talked about lighthearted things.

"Tell me something about you I don't know," he said while eating his General Tso's chicken.

"Hmm." She thought about things she'd learned about herself after she'd left foster care. Uplifting things. "Oh, I know! I found out that my sisters and I were named after things in the solar system."

"Really?"

She nodded. "It's one of the things my mom told her when Aunt Joy found out about us. Apparently, before her parents threw my mother out and things went bad, Mom was smart. She loved science. I was named after the outermost moon of Saturn, Halley for Halley's Comet, and Juliette for a moon of Uranus."

"Fascinating," he said. "Seriously."

"What about you? Tell me something I don't know about you."

"Hmm. Well, there's this. Prison left me claustrophobic."

She blinked, lowering the chopsticks into a box of food. "Jake, I had no idea. When you reacted that way to the small bedroom, I didn't realize."

He shrugged. "It was a dark room in that house and small. No reason to willingly put myself in a place I'm uncomfortable. This apartment is small but it's bright, with a lot of windows. That was a requirement and it's why the house I love works so well. The view of nature and the trees... nothing like a dark, damp cell."

On impulse, she reached over and pulled him into her arms, offering him what she could, comfort and warmth.

He hugged her back. "It's fine. I wasn't looking to bring you down. Just offering some insight," he said, pulling back.

She wouldn't dwell on it if he didn't want to, so she merely smiled and said, "Well, I'm glad you shared it with me."

Then she began cleaning up, determined to get home before she did something stupid, like fall into bed with him again. Because he was just so easy to be with, to like, to keep falling harder for.

She was tying up the full garbage bag when he came up behind her, wrapping his arms around her waist. She jumped and backed away from the pail. "What are you doing?"

"What I've been dying to do since the last time I had my hands on you. Holding you in my arms." He spun her around so they were face-to-face and her heart began to race.

"Jake—"

He nuzzled his face into her neck, and her knees went weak along with her will to do anything but yield to his touch. Her hands came to his neck and she threaded them through his hair, leaning into him, her breasts brushing against his chest.

"See? Giving in isn't such a bad thing."

At the moment, she agreed with him. He reached for her jacket and peeled it off her shoulders, laying it on the counter. Next he grasped the hem of her camisole and slid it over her head, leaving her in her skirt and lace bra.

She pulled his shirt up and off, adding the tee to the same pile as her clothes. She ran her hands up his chest, feeling his warmth and strength against her palms.

"I love your hair down," he said, reaching up and tugging at the bun she'd made this morning.

In a split second, her professional look was gone, her hair tumbling around her shoulders. "That's better," he said, sifting his fingers through the strands and tugging on her scalp in an erotically delicious way.

His hands came to the waistband of her skirt at the

e time she reached for the button on his jeans. In seconds they were both undressed, him shedding his boxer briefs with the denim, her wearing only her bra and panties.

"You are so fucking beautiful," he said in a gruff voice.

Her cheeks heated at his blatant perusal. "You make me feel that way." She let her gaze slide over his body, his thick erection standing at attention.

She reached for him, but he caught her hand, bringing it back down to her side. "You don't want this over before it begins."

So she waited and was rewarded when he brushed his thumbs over her nipples, the buds hardening beneath the thin lace. He quickly removed her bra, unhooking the back and sliding the garment off her shoulders. Then, looping his fingers into her panties, he removed them next, taking the time to slide her heels off her feet as well.

She stood naked in his kitchen, completely bared to him and totally aroused.

"I would have left those sexy shoes on, but for what I have planned, you'll need your balance."

"Ooh, do tell."

He grinned, a sexy grin that made her wet, and then turned her around facing the island counter before placing a firm hand on her back and bending her over, her breasts pressing against the cold Formica top.

Arousal pounded through her veins as she turned her head to the side and met his gaze. "What's your plan?"

He slid a finger along her spine, her back arching, her sex pulsing with need. He hooked a foot around her ankle and spread her legs wider. "There. Perfect," he said, cupping her ass in his hand.

"Jake," she said in a trembling voice, her body soft and ready for his.

"Don't move. I'll be right back," he said in a voice she intended to obey.

He disappeared for a few seconds, seconds in which the wait merely heightened her excitement and need. He returned and she heard the crinkle of a condom wrapper, then a groan as he probably pulled it on.

Meanwhile, she was bent over the counter, ass in the air, waiting for whatever came next, taking in shaky, excited breaths of air.

"Now this is a sight." He cupped one cheek in his hand, squeezing it.

She arched into him, wanting nothing more than for him to fill her.

He came up behind her, his cock at her entrance, her body clenching with need. And then he thrust deep, taking her completely. She gasped at his intrusion, the feeling of him thick and heavy inside her sending spirals of intense sensation rocketing through her.

"Jesus, you're tight from this angle. You feel so damned good."

She wriggled around him, squeezing her core around his shaft. "Is that a deliberate tease?" he asked.

"No, it's a needy wiggle," she muttered. "Now move."

He swatted her behind and chuckled. "Relax and let me set the pace. I guarantee you'll appreciate it later."

She laughed.

Had she ever laughed during sex before? Relaxed enough to have fun and enjoy the moment instead of rushing to get it over with? Yeah. With Jake, she thought, as he began to do as she asked. And move.

He drove into her, his hands holding her hips, as he took her over and over, her body flying higher with every shift of his hips against hers.

Her body answered his rhythm, and she began to soar, the small contractions racking her body growing stronger with every thrust. She shook and trembled as she grew closer to a climax, which he pulled from her with the next plunge of his thick cock into her sex.

"Jake!" She cried out his name as her orgasm

struck, waves of glorious pleasure swamping her.

Her climax triggered his, and he groaned, taking her hard, over and over until he collapsed against her, his large body crushing hers while they caught their breath.

A few minutes later, he pulled out of her, and she felt the loss, her body damp and sated. She reached for her clothes and they dressed in silence. It wasn't uncomfortable, but she felt herself withdrawing, pulling into herself, the old fear returning.

Don't, she instructed. *Just enjoy what you have and don't feel regret. Just protect your heart.*

She only hoped she could follow her own advice, because every time she was with Jake, she lost more pieces of herself to him.

JAKE PUT AN offer in on the ranch house he'd fallen in love with, and after a few days of negotiations, he'd gotten his house. The current owners were eager to sell and retire down south and it hadn't been difficult to work out a deal. He'd be signing the contract in a few days and close in a month. It was fast, but he was excited to move in and had already started making plans for changes he wanted to do in the house.

He called Phoebe during the week and asked her to help him pick furniture for the kids' rooms, since he wanted those ready as soon as he moved in. That and the master bedroom. The rest he'd take from his apartment and buy as needed.

Today he was going to pick up Callie to go over to Jamie's baseball game, then introduce his two kids. His stomach twisted with nerves but he was sure it'd be okay. They were both good-hearted children. Things would work out.

He pulled up to Lindsay's house and climbed out of the car to collect Callie. He'd taken the extra car he kept for when he had his daughter since he couldn't put her car seat in the truck.

He rang the bell and Lindsay answered the door. "Jake, she'll be ready in a minute. Come on in," she said, sounding subdued.

Stepping inside, he looked at his ex. "Can we talk?"

"Sure. I wanted to ask you something, too."

He nodded. "Ladies first."

She sighed. "Fine. Dad told me you bought a house."

He narrowed his gaze, wondering what her issue was with his purchase. "I did. I figured with two kids, it was time to find something bigger."

She winced at the *two kids* remark. Well, tough. She'd have to get used to it. "I just thought, as long as you were renting, that maybe one day…" She shook her head. "Never mind."

He wasn't about to push her to finish that sentence. Not for a million dollars did he want to hear how she'd hoped they'd get back together.

"Anyway, what did you want to talk about?" she asked when he didn't pick up on her comment.

"I'm taking Callie to meet her brother today and I wanted you to know."

Lindsay's cheeks flushed and she clenched her jaw. "Half brother and don't you think it's a little soon?"

He shook his head. "He's her *brother*, since I don't intend on drawing distinctions between my children, and no, I don't think it's too soon. They're kids and they adapt easily. Much easier than adults, apparently," he muttered, knowing he should have kept his sarcasm to himself but unable to deal with her drama today.

"That's unfair, Jake. You spring the fact that you have a child with the woman you loved before me and you expect me to just… What did you say? Adapt?"

He counted to five in his head before answering, calming himself down. "Since you won't have to see or deal with Phoebe or Jamie"—at least as little as he could manage it—"I'm not sure why it matters to you now. Our daughter is a champ. She'll take the news in stride. If anything, she'll be excited to have a sibling to hang with sometimes."

Tears filled her eyes. "You don't get it," she said, folding her arms across her chest.

"Actually I do," he said, softening his voice. "And I'm sorry this hurts you, but it wasn't planned. It wasn't a secret I kept from you. It's something I told you about as soon as I knew it myself."

He paused, letting that sink in.

"So I'd appreciate it if we could all be adults and not take it out on the kids. Be nice if Callie tells you about Jamie. And if you ever meet him, be more like the woman I married." He reached out and squeezed her arm. "You can handle it, Lindsay. We're over. You should be moving on," he said gently.

She didn't reply, all but ignoring his request. Which didn't mean she wouldn't do as he asked, just that she wasn't going to make anything easy. No big surprise there, he thought, frustrated with her as usual.

"Is Callie going to be with Phoebe?" Lindsay asked.

He wished to God he could lie and avoid this answer. "Yes. I'm taking her to Jamie's baseball game."

She glared at him through damp eyes. "Callie, your father is here!" she called out instead of replying.

"Daddy!" Callie rushed to him, dressed adorably in a pair of pink bike shorts that matched her cast and a tee shirt with a bow on the back. Her hair was pulled up in pigtails, and she wore her huge smile on her face. She had a matching pink backpack with what he assumed had her iPad to play with. Although it hadn't been his idea to get her such an expensive item, Brent had bought her one at Lindsay's insistence. "I'm ready!" she said.

"Me, too, munchkin. Kiss Mommy good-bye and let's get going."

"Bye, Mommy!" She put her little arms around Lindsay's neck.

"Bye, baby. Be good for Daddy and have fun." She hugged her and sent her on her way.

On their way to the field, Jake explained to her that they were going to a baseball game, where she was going to meet her brother and Phoebe, in terms she could understand.

"Yay!" was her reply.

Why couldn't adults be as easy as children?

Chapter Nine

P HOEBE SET UP her folding chair on the grass on the first base line with the other parents to watch Jamie's baseball game. The boys were already huddled near the makeshift dugout, talking to their coach.

She'd brought extra chairs for Jake and Callie, grateful that today Halley and Kane had opted not to join them. Of course, the fact that she hadn't told her sister Jake was coming might have helped. They rarely missed a game, and she didn't hold it against her sister. It was sweet of her to show up for Jamie as much as she did.

She bit her lip nervously as she waited for them to arrive, making conversation with the other parents, not addressing the fact that it was Jamie's dad she was waiting for and not her sister. They'd be talking about it soon enough. Not that she cared. She just didn't feel close enough with any of them to discuss her personal situation.

Finally, she saw Jake walking onto the field, holding hands with an adorable little girl in pigtails. She hadn't seen Callie that day in the hospital, so today was a big day for them all.

She waited for him to reach her before rising from her chair. "Hi!"

"Hi." He leaned in and kissed her cheek, taking her by surprise. "Callie, I want you to meet someone."

The little girl hugged her father's leg. "Callie, this is Phoebe, Jamie's mommy. Remember I told you about her in the car on the way here?"

Callie nodded and looked up at Phoebe.

Phoebe dropped to one knee, getting onto her level. "Hi, Callie. It's nice to meet you."

"Hi." She smiled and Phoebe noticed her teeth were still growing in.

"Thank you for coming to watch the game," Phoebe said. "Do you want to come sit?"

Callie nodded and Phoebe rose to her feet. "I brought fold-up chairs for you both," she told Jake.

"Thank you." He smiled at her and held out his hand for Callie. "Come on. Let's go watch the game."

They settled into chairs, Callie with an iPad in her lap. Luckily they were in the shade and she could see the screen, which kept her busy while the game went on.

"She's adorable," Phoebe told Jake, who grinned

and clearly agreed. She was also well behaved considering how... well, boring a boy's baseball game could be for a girl her age.

Jake seemed preoccupied. Although he paid attention to the game, splitting his time between watching his son and answering Callie's never-ending questions, he seemed weighted down, like he had something on his mind.

Phoebe waited until Callie seemed occupied with her game on the other side of Jake before asking, "Hey, is everything okay?"

He nodded. "Just the usual uncomfortable conversation with Lindsay," he whispered, not facing Callie.

Phoebe's stomach knotted at the mention of his ex-wife and her shenanigans. "What happened?"

"Nothing out of the ordinary. She found out I was buying a house, and I think it dashed some dreams she still held on to as long as I was renting and didn't have a house that I *owned*." He frowned as he recalled the conversation.

Phoebe couldn't help but wonder why Lindsay was holding on if Jake made it as clear as he claimed that it was over. It seemed extreme and unhealthy. But it wasn't her place to say, especially with Callie right here.

"I also explained to her that, as far as I'm concerned, Jamie and Callie are equally my children and she'd best adjust quickly and learn to be civil regardless of the circumstances. Don't worry, she heard me," he said, obviously addressing Phoebe's concerns about Lindsay and how she might treat Jamie.

"Okay, I'm glad you had the conversation," she said diplomatically.

But his mood made it clear something hadn't gone well between them, which fired up all Phoebe's worries.

Just then, Jamie came up to bat.

"Go, Jamie!" Phoebe yelled, clapping her hands for her son. "He usually strikes out," she whispered.

"Although I only worked with him once, I taught him about keeping an eye on the ball and not swinging if it looks too high or too low. So let's see," Jake said.

Jamie swung and missed. Strike. Another swing and miss. Strike. Ball, which impressed Phoebe because he'd never let one pass before, and another swing and miss for a strike. She blew out a frustrated breath.

"That's okay, buddy!" she yelled. "He'll hit next time," she said hopefully.

"I'll definitely work with him before his next game," Jake said, and when he made the promise, Phoebe believed him.

Afterwards, they made introductions between Jamie and Callie, which went well. Then Jake suggested pizza for dinner, and everyone left the field smiling, even Jamie, whose team had lost the game.

A WEEK AFTER the baseball game, Jake wrapped up the Renault job, and he was meeting Phoebe for a final walk-through of the house and renovations. Then he could let Brent know things were completed on time, within budget, and the owner had signed off.

He'd seen Phoebe during the week, to turn over the signed contracts for the house he was buying. He'd also managed to do the inspection quickly thanks to the connections he had in the business, and the house didn't hold any surprises despite its age, and he would be closing at the end of the month.

House business aside, he and Phoebe hadn't been alone since they'd been together at his apartment, and though she hadn't pulled back, she wasn't all in, either. He had no doubt she was withholding, not telling him everything that was on her mind when it came to their relationship, and he didn't know how to push her for answers that she wasn't willing to give.

Was it Lindsay? He had no doubt his ex-wife's behavior played a part in her reluctance to commit, but it wasn't the sole reason Phoebe had doubts and fears about them. He wasn't giving up, either.

Phoebe walked into the house at nine a.m. sharp.

Unlike the baseball game, where he'd gotten to see her body in fitted jeans and a white tee shirt, which molded to her curves, today she was back in her workweek power suit. He liked both versions of the woman and was happy to see her regardless of what she wore.

"Good morning," she said, clearly in a good mood.

"Good morning to you." Refusing to keep things strictly professional when they were alone, he leaned in and kissed her on the lips.

She stiffened in surprise, but instead of backing away, she kissed him back, something he took as a positive sign.

They'd had a good night at Jamie's baseball game. Callie had been happy around Phoebe, who'd made an effort to talk to his daughter, even getting down on her level to make her feel comfortable. His heart had warmed at the sight.

"Are you ready to do the walk-through?" he asked.

She nodded. "I have my cell phone so I can take pictures to send to Celeste. I have no doubt she's going to be thrilled, but let's see."

He led her from the front door, showing her the trim touch-ups, to the kitchen, the bathrooms, and everything in between that he, his men, and the subcontractors had worked on. She paused to take photos and constantly reiterated her praise and appreciation for the job he'd done. And by the time they were finished, he knew he could tell Brent the work was complete.

They were in the kitchen when Phoebe turned to him. "I have the final paperwork for you on your house, signed by the sellers. It's in my car."

He nodded. "Great. I'll walk out with you."

He locked up the house and followed Phoebe to her car. She leaned over to pull out the contract, giving him a nice view of her rounded ass, causing his cock to swell inside his pants.

He cleared his throat as she rose and handed him the papers. "Looks like I'll own the house by the end of the month," he said, excited by the prospect of moving out of his small apartment and into a real home.

"That's the plan."

"So what's on tap for the rest of the day?" he asked.

She frowned at the question. "Paperwork, paperwork, and more paperwork," she muttered. "Why?"

"What do you say to playing hooky and going furniture shopping? I'm a guy and it's not my specialty. Take pity on me and help me out?"

"I thought we had plans for next week?"

They did but he was anxious to go, not that he'd go without her. He had a reason for wanting to make her a part of the process of decorating his new home and not just because he needed the help. Which he did. But if he had his way, she'd be helping to pick out things for a house she'd be living in one day.

No, it wasn't as large or as grand as the guesthouse where she lived now with his son, but it was small and cozy. It would be renovated to her taste and specs. But most importantly, it would be a *home*.

He had a ways to go to get her to come around, but he was nothing if not persistent.

"I'm free today, and the sooner I order, the sooner they'll be able to deliver, hopefully the first week I move in."

"Hmm. Can't really argue with that. Okay," she said. "I'll go with you today."

He let out a relieved breath. "Great. Because I need new everything, from a bed and bedroom furniture to a family room set. Can you call and see if we can stop by and do some measuring?"

She rolled her eyes. "You really did set me up for this," she said but she smiled at his enthusiasm. "Give me a few minutes to call the seller and see if we can stop by. I take it you have a tape measure?"

"I'm a contractor, aren't I?" He always had one handy in his truck.

An hour later, they'd dropped her car off at her house. Then they took measurements of all the rooms he wanted to furnish immediately in the new house, and they were on their way to furniture stores in the neighboring town because Rosewood Bay didn't have any large chains.

They started in a mattress store, which was his priority.

"Don't you have a mattress?" she asked.

"It's a garbage one. Kills my back. I was in a rush to move out and I ordered over the phone. I'm going to test them out this time."

"Okay," she said, following him to the higher-end mattresses at the far end of the store.

He stopped at a pillow-top that was on sale, and he patted the top. "Nice. Check it out," he said, telling himself they'd be spending a lot of time on whatever mattress he chose.

Hey, a man could be confident, right?

"What? No. It's your bed. You try it out."

"I want your opinion," he said, raising an eyebrow in what was almost a dare.

She rolled her eyes. "Fine." She kicked off her heels and lay down on the bed, groaning in pleasure as her body molded against the pillow-top. "This is a nice bed."

"Really? Let's see." Before she could pop up, he lay down beside her, stretching out his body to test the mattress. "You're right. This is a fantastic bed," he said, turning his head toward her, meeting her gaze.

"You should check out a few others," she suggested, not getting up from her comfortable position.

"Why? I like this one."

"What if you like another one better?" she asked, ever the voice of reason.

"Do you like this one?" He reached out and threaded his fingers through hers.

Her lashes fluttered over her green eyes. "Why does that matter?"

Oh, fuck it. In for a penny, he thought. "Because I plan on spending a hell of a lot of time with you in this bed. I want you to be comfortable."

Her cheeks turned a healthy shade of red and he laughed. "Well?"

"I like the bed," she said, her voice husky with desire.

"Can I help you folks?" a salesman asked.

Phoebe scrambled to sit upright in the bed.

Jake braced a hand beneath his head and glanced up at the man. "I'll take this one," he said, doing his best not to grin.

ONE THING PHOEBE learned about Jake during their day of shopping, he didn't take long to make up his mind. Once she'd found something she liked, he'd agreed and hadn't needed to see anything more. So the hours passed relatively quickly as they shifted their attention from room to room in his new house, stopping for lunch at a restaurant near the main road where all the stores were located. By the time the day ended, Jake had a houseful of furniture ordered and she was exhausted.

Phoebe discovered something else today, too. She was beginning to believe Jake wanted something serious with her. Something real and meaningful, and he had the patience not only to go after what he wanted but to wait until she was ready. Of course, that didn't mean he wouldn't do everything he could to convince her of his intentions.

She wasn't stupid. The fact that he'd taken her along for his furniture, that he'd made sure she was comfortable in his bed, all went a long way toward mellowing out her and her fears.

So when he pulled up to her house to drop her off, she took herself by surprise. "Jake, my sister and Kane are having a small get-together at her beach house this weekend. Would you like to come with me?"

A slow, sexy smile curved his lips. "I would. And I'm glad you asked me."

He leaned in, placed a hand behind her neck, and pulled her to him for a kiss. His lips sealed over hers, his tongue gliding over the seam, and next thing she knew, the kiss was hot, him devouring her where they sat.

"What was that for?" she asked, breathless after they'd parted.

"That was my thank you for taking a day out of your work week to come shopping with me. It was because I like being with you. And to let you know I want to be with you in the future."

She forced herself to relax at his words because that was her new plan. To see where things led but to be very careful with her heart.

"Okay then," she whispered, said heart beating hard inside her chest. "Jamie will be home from camp in an hour if you want to stay."

"I wish I could, but I have to go by the office before closing, then I'm having dinner with Brent." He shot her a regret-filled look. "Another time, though."

"Sure."

He hopped out of the truck and walked her to her door, seeing her inside before striding back to his vehicle.

Once he was gone, she leaned against the door and prayed she was being smart. She couldn't freeze him out; he was too tempting. Too sweet. Too everything. And he wasn't giving her a reason to hold on to her fears.

So she'd released her hold on them. A little bit.

✧ ✧ ✧

THE DAY OF the gathering at Halley's was sunny and bright, a warm summer day. Jake picked up Phoebe to go to her sister's, and as he pulled up and climbed out of the car, Jamie ran out of the house to meet him.

"Dad! Can we practice baseball again?"

Jake had come by one evening after camp and worked with Jamie on hitting the ball. After one lesson, he was connecting more often and Jake was proud of him. He was a quick learner.

"Sorry but we're going to your Aunt Halley's, remember?"

His shoulders sagged in disappointment. "Yeah. I just thought we could get some practice in first."

"I know but then you'll be all sweaty and your mom won't be happy with us, right?"

He nodded. "She's almost ready. She's just getting some cookies she baked ready to go."

"I'm right here." Phoebe walked out of the house with a Tupperware full of cookies in her hands.

She was dressed completely differently than he'd ever seen her in a sundress with bright-colored flowers as the pattern. Her hair was in a high ponytail, and sunglasses were perched on top of her head.

She looked fresh, young, and beautiful, and his heart swelled as he gazed at her. "You look amazing," he said, unable to keep the words in.

She beamed at him. "Thank you. I've been waiting for an excuse to wear this dress. Jamie, can you hold the cookies while I lock up the house?" She handed him the tub.

They drove across town to the beach, where Jake was once again struck by the wealth in the family. To own a house directly on the water, and one as large and as beautiful as her sister's... well, it was something.

He didn't dwell on their differences, though. Phoebe had never indicated anything like that mattered to her, and it damn well didn't make a difference to him.

"Her house is beautiful," he said as they pulled up and parked out front.

"Aunt Joy bought it for her a couple of years ago. Halley went through some... stuff in foster care and needed a place where she could be alone and paint. This place is good for her."

They headed around the back, where a wide deck wrapped around the outside of the house, and they walked up the side stairs.

"Kane finished the deck for Halley last summer," Phoebe said as they climbed up where the party was located. "Stick close and I'll introduce you to the people you don't know."

It looked like a small group, he thought, as Phoebe

brought him over to say hello to Halley first, who was talking to a pretty woman with wavy brown hair.

"Hi, guys," Phoebe said.

"Hi! So glad you're here!" Halley pulled her sister into a hug. "And Jake, it's good to see you again."

"Same here," he said to her. "Thanks for having me."

Halley smiled. "Of course." She dismissed his thanks easily. "Jake, this is Andrea Harmon, Kane's sister. Andrea, meet Jake Nichols."

He shook her hand.

"Is Nicky here?" Jamie asked.

Andrea smiled. "He's down by the water with his grandpa."

"You can run down. I'll keep an eye on you until you get to them," Phoebe said.

Jamie took off down the steps again, headed for the beach. Jake watched until he saw him catch up with an older man and a boy who, from a distance, appeared shorter than Jamie.

"Nicky is Andrea's seven—"

"Now eight," Andrea interrupted.

Phoebe smiled. "Her eight-year-old son."

"Got it," Jake said.

Kane was talking to another man, and Jake didn't want Phoebe to feel like she had to babysit him. "Why don't you hang out with your sister. I'll go talk to

Kane," he said.

She nodded and he headed in the direction of the two men.

"Grab a beer," Kane said before Jake met up with them, pointing to a cooler in the corner.

He pulled out a cold bottle and joined them. Kane introduced him to Jackson Traynor, who worked for him at his garage.

They talked sports for a little while, until Jackson got a phone call and had to go, leaving Jake and Kane to hang out while the women still talked across the deck.

"I hear you're buying a house in Rosewood Bay," Kane said. He tilted his head toward Halley. "The women talked. Get used to it," he said, laughing.

Jake grinned. "I can handle it."

"I understand you and Phoebe go way back."

"Way, way back," he said. "We were kids when she got pregnant." He shook his head. "I'd give anything to have been there."

Kane smiled grimly. "Neither sister had it easy. Halley was withdrawn before I met up with her again, nursing her pain, while Phoebe likes to go through life as if nothing gets to her. But it's not true."

This man knew the women well. "I'm still trying to work out what's eating Phoebe half the time," he said, agreeing with Kane. "She's not opening up."

"It'll be worth it once she does," Kane assured him, tipping his bottle and tapping Kane's with his.

Just then the boys came running up the stairs, Kane's father trudging behind them.

"They wear you out, Dad?" Kane asked.

"I can keep up with 'em," the older man said, but from the worn look on his face, he'd had it.

Kane chuckled. "I see that Halley's aunt is here, which means this party can get underway."

Curious, Jake tipped his head to the side. "Am I missing something?" he asked.

Kane leaned against the railing. "Nope. It's a surprise, even for Halley. Just wish me luck," he said, straightening as he shoved one hand into his front pocket. With the other, he rid himself of his beer bottle, placing it on the railing.

"Attention, everyone," Kane said, striding over to where Halley stood.

The people on the deck gathered around, whispering and curious.

Jake set his beer on the railing beside Kane's and made his way to Phoebe. Listening to his gut, he wrapped an arm around her waist, pulling her close. She hesitated before leaning into him, her lithe, warm body easing against his.

Kane stood in front of Halley. "I debated doing this when we were alone, but then I decided you deserved to have the people you love surrounding you when I asked."

Beside him, Phoebe gasped. Halley did the same, her hands coming to cover her mouth, her surprise evident.

"When I answered a call for a tow last summer, something I rarely do anymore because Jackson usually handles things, little did I know I had something special waiting for me. Or maybe I should say someone special." He paused, then went on. "I sensed something special about you back in high school, and I knew when I found you on the side of the road that I had to get to know you better. Since then, I've wanted nothing more than to be by your side."

Phoebe sniffed and Jake held her closer, knowing how emotional it had to be for her to watch the sister she loved getting engaged.

"Kane," Halley whispered.

"Shh, baby. I'm not finished. I waited for you to be ready to date me, and I waited for you to be ready for me to move in, and I waited some more until you were ready for this next step. I decided I've waited long enough."

Everyone laughed at that, as Kane pulled something out of his shorts pocket and dropped to one knee. "Halley Ward, will you do me the honor of becoming my wife?"

"Oh my God, Kane. Yes. Yes!" He slipped the ring on her finger and she threw herself into his arms.

Even Jake had a lump in his throat at the sight, and Phoebe was a sniffling mess beside him.

He hugged her to him. "It's a good thing," he reminded her.

"I know," she said, still crying.

"Go congratulate her." He squeezed her once and let her go, watching as she wrapped her arms around first her sister, then Kane.

His girl had a big heart. And like Halley, she had fears she hadn't yet conquered. Like Kane, Jake planned to be there every step of the way, because the man had a valid point.

These sisters were worth the wait.

Chapter Ten

THE NEXT MONTH passed in a blur of work and summer activity. Phoebe saw Jake a few times a week because he came by to help Jamie with his baseball skills, and she'd invite him to stay for dinner. They ate meals like a family, and she had to admit it warmed her heart. But she didn't let him stay over, despite him having asked, a number of times. She didn't want to send the wrong statement to Jamie, that his parents were together in any permanent way. She wasn't ready for that, was still protecting her heart by holding back from Jake. It wasn't fair but she couldn't help it.

Other than that, life was quiet and good. She was almost afraid to jinx it.

Jake closed on his house and he was moving in this weekend. He'd hired a moving truck for the heavy items he was keeping from his apartment, sold things like the bed, and given things away to Goodwill. He wanted to start fresh in the new house and she didn't blame him. She saw many Target runs in his future.

She and Jamie promised to stop by and help him where they could. Jamie was excited to see his room, though she explained to him the furniture and bed hadn't yet been delivered and wouldn't be for another week or so. Jake had to schedule the date with the store.

She threw on a pair of exercise shorts and a tee shirt, knowing she'd get sweaty helping him with the clothes and things he'd loaded onto hangers in his truck, and she and Jamie set off for his new place.

The moving truck was in the driveway behind Jake's loaded truck.

"Don't get in the way," she warned Jamie. "The movers will be busy with heavy furniture.

"I know, Mom. But Dad said I could help."

She laughed. "I'm sure you will."

"Dad!" he yelled and ran off in the direction of Jake's truck.

She still wasn't used to him saying that word. To him having a father. His real father. She got goose bumps whenever he spoke of Jake in that reverent tone, and she thanked her lucky stars that she'd run into him that day, more for her boy than for herself. Okay a little for herself, too. It was becoming easier to think that way.

They spent the entire day helping him unpack. Despite his arguing that he just wanted the company, Phoebe had no problem doing her bit, working on organizing his closet, because the way he'd brought the clothing on hangers... well there was no rhyme or reason to where anything was located. The neat freak in her couldn't leave the dangling shirts and jeans.

Jamie never left Jake's side, mirroring his actions, helping in any way he could, basically looking for his father's approval and attention, which Jake gave to him in spades.

Finally, Jake declared they'd done all they could for the day, and he ordered pizza in via delivery. Phoebe was hungry and happy to get off her feet, so she plopped down beside a box they were using as a makeshift table. Because he'd bought a new one of those, yet to be delivered, as well.

Jake was grabbing silverware from a marked box in the kitchen when the pizza arrived, and Jamie, contrary to everything Phoebe had taught him, ran for the door, swinging it open without asking who was there.

Phoebe rushed up behind him, only to find Lindsay standing on the other side. "Lindsay."

"You."

Phoebe lightly grasped Jamie's arm and moved him out of the way. The lecture on waiting for a grown-up and asking who was at the door would have to wait.

"Jamie, go get Jake from the kitchen, please," she said, eager to get her son away from a gutted-looking Lindsay.

"I came to see Jake."

"Hello to you, too, Lindsay." Somehow she was determined to get through to this woman that she was rude. And they didn't have to be enemies. "Don't you think it's time we talked?" Phoebe asked.

"I have nothing to say to you." Lindsay pushed past her and let herself into the house like she belonged there at the same time Jake came out from the kitchen, Jamie tagging along after him.

"You have company," Phoebe said to Jake. "Jamie, come into the other room with me." She refused to subject him to an unpredictable Lindsay.

"Where's Callie?" Jake asked Lindsay.

He didn't ask Phoebe to stay. They both must be in agreement that protecting Jamie came first. Which didn't mean Phoebe didn't wish she could remain in the room and stake her claim.

"Callie's with my dad. We were having dinner and I saw a note on his calendar that you were moving in today. With the address scribbled on the side."

Phoebe could no longer see what was happening, but she could still hear, and though the proper thing to do would be to step away so she wasn't eavesdropping, she couldn't bring herself to do it.

"What are you doing here?" he asked her.

"I wanted to see your new place. To see if you needed help with anything." Her voice sounded shaky to Phoebe's ears.

"Mom? Who is that?" Jamie asked.

She touched his shoulder. "That's Callie's mom, honey."

"Oh." He bit down on his bottom lip, obviously unsure of what to make of the situation.

Join the club, Phoebe thought. She grasped on to the doorframe, the kitchen out of sight of the family room.

But whatever Jake said next to Lindsay was quiet and soft.

In deference to her delicate feelings? Or because he really just felt bad for her and he didn't want to see her hurt anymore?

She heard more whispering and then the sound of the door closing.

She shut her eyes and sighed, tired of Lindsay's attempts at drawing Jake back in.

"Come in," Jake called out.

Jamie rushed past Phoebe and headed straight for the pizza. "I'm starving," he said and grabbed a paper plate and a slice and settled onto the floor to eat.

Jake met Phoebe's gaze. "Sorry about that. She has a hard time accepting things the way they are."

Phoebe swallowed hard and nodded. "She has a hard time being polite, too." She glanced at Jamie, but he was too busy picking out the next large slice of pizza to care what the grown-ups were saying.

"I'm not going to make excuses for her. She's never had to share me before." He winced as soon as the words escaped his mouth, but for Phoebe it was too late.

"Is that what we're doing? Sharing you?" she asked, annoyed with his poor word choice.

She looked again at Jamie, who was now chugging a bottle of water, still not paying the least bit of attention to them.

"Phoebe, that's not what I meant and you know it."

"I do know but it was a stupid thing to say. And frankly I'm tired of her attitude. I tried to have a conversation with her, but she wasn't having any of it."

He looked uncomfortable. "I know. I wish I could change it but I can't. Believe me, I'll have another talk with her."

Phoebe shook her head. "I'd rather you didn't. It won't make a difference." She was just going to have to get used to dealing with Lindsay if she wanted Jake in her life.

She wished it wasn't so hard. Every time Lindsay

pushed her way in, Phoebe was forced to deal with the reminder of life's uncertainties. That just because she and Jake were together now, there was no guarantee for the future. Her past had taught her that.

She'd been holding back from him for that very reason, and she knew he was being patient, but how long would that understanding last?

JAKE CLEANED UP after Phoebe and Jamie left, beyond annoyed that their dinner and an enjoyable day even with the move had been interrupted by Lindsay. The woman was even more persistent than he'd given her credit for, and that was saying something. In the years since the divorce, she'd pulled stunts like having him come over for leaky pipes, but she'd never interfered in his personal life in a way that caused trouble. She had to have known there was a good chance Phoebe would be over. She knew they had a relationship now, yet she was still making her play as if there were a chance for their future.

He hated to pull her father into his personal life, but he was thinking he might not have a choice but to go to Brent and ask him to weigh in with his daughter. She usually listened to her father, and that was the only alternative Jake could see in order to get her to back off. He had to do something. Phoebe was losing patience with Lindsay's antics and he didn't blame her.

As for Phoebe, it was obvious to Jake that she was present in the relationship, enjoying what they shared—for now. But he didn't sense that she was as invested as he was in a future. She held back when any conversation came up about things getting more serious. She didn't want him staying over at night because it might send the wrong example to Jamie.

What? That their parents were in love?

Because he damn well loved her. Never mind that he always had. In the last month plus, he'd gotten to know the woman she was now. Strong, brave, kind, and giving. How could he not love who she'd become, as well?

But he hadn't told her, because he sensed an innate skittishness when it came to them that she hadn't been able to shake. He didn't think the Lindsay situation helped, but it wasn't the root cause. It merely exacerbated whatever fears she refused to share with him.

He was frustrated and at his wits' end with what to do in order to get where he wanted to be in his life—with Phoebe, invested for the long haul.

PHOEBE HAD THE morning free, no appointments or clients, so she drove to her sister's beach house for an unscheduled visit. She didn't miss the irony that she was turning to her younger sister for advice, the same sister who, one year ago, couldn't get her own relationship on track. But Halley was now blissfully happy with Kane, and maybe Phoebe could learn a thing or two from her.

She rang the doorbell, and her sister answered, wearing what Phoebe called her painting dress, the one she wore when she was lost in her work.

"I'm sorry. I'm interrupting you."

Halley waved a hand. "Don't be silly. I'm never too busy for you. Come on in." She stepped back and Phoebe walked into the house.

They headed to the kitchen, where Phoebe snagged a can of Diet Coke from the refrigerator and popped the top. She took a long sip.

"So. What'd you do to Jake now?" Halley asked.

Phoebe coughed on the bubbles. "What makes you think it was me?"

Halley laughed. "I don't. I took a wild guess. It's either you or his ex. The man seems pretty perfect to me."

Settling herself into a chair at the table, Phoebe rolled her eyes at her sister. "Whose side are you on?"

"Always yours. What happened?"

"It's me. I'm having trouble dealing with his relationship with his ex-wife. It's not that I'm jealous or that I think he loves her, but there's a connection there that I'm clearly coming between."

Halley frowned. "On Lindsay's end, maybe. Not on Jake's. He told Kane how much he's struggling to get inside your head." She glanced at Phoebe. "What's going on?"

"I'm still trying to shake the past." She sighed and leaned an arm on the table. "You know, it's funny. Not ha-ha funny, but funny that I'm the one who had a good foster care experience, I'm the one who told you to give Kane a chance, and yet here I am now, afraid to go all in and risk my heart."

Halley settled into the chair next to her and took her hand. "I can't tell you what to do. I can't convince you that love is worth the risk if you're not ready to believe it yourself. But I can tell you being alone, by choice because you're afraid, hurts just as much if not more than taking a risk and actually getting hurt."

"Says my wise younger sister."

"Says your more experienced sister. I've been there, remember? I let Kane go and it was the worst time of my life."

Phoebe blew out a breath. "I remember and I thought you were crazy for doing it. Now? I under-stand self-protection."

"Only you can get past it. I support you no matter what you decide. You know that."

"I do and I appreciate it." Of all people, Phoebe

knew her sister would have her back.

"Have you talked to Jake about what's scaring you? Did you tell him you're skittish about commitment because you're afraid somehow you're going to lose him and be hurt later on?"

She shook her head. "I'm afraid he won't understand. He's been through so much worse than me, and he's got his head on straight and he's so steady and together."

"Phoebe, you of all people should know that could be a cover. You walk around like you rule the world. Who would know you still have scars from the past? He'd want to be there to get you through it."

"Or he'll think I'm crazy," she said, laughing. "I feel like I need to get through this on my own."

Halley sighed, her frustration obvious. "Okay, fine. I'll just change the subject."

"I'd like that."

Halley leaned closer, elbow on the table. "I've been thinking about Juliette a lot lately. Especially since Kane and I got engaged." She held out her hand, displaying her ring, a huge grin on her face at the sight of it. "I wish she could be here for my wedding," she said, smile fading.

"I know. Me, too." Phoebe pulled Halley into a hug. "But you have me. And you can bet I'll make sure everything is perfect. Have you and Kane made any plans yet?"

Halley shook her head. "We're just enjoying the newness of being engaged. We'll talk about it soon, I'm sure."

"Just tell me what you need me to do and I'm there for you." She couldn't wait to help plan her sister's wedding. She deserved all the happiness she could find, and Kane was so good to her. "Well, I should get going and leave you to paint."

"Are you sure? We can talk some more if you want."

Phoebe shook her head. "I think I'll go to the office and do some work. I'm better off keeping busy."

"Okay. Just remember something, okay?"

She tipped her head to one side, waiting.

"You deserve love and happiness. But only you can open yourself up to those things and let them in."

Phoebe smiled at her sister's words. "Yes, wise one. I will take it all under advisement."

With a laugh, Halley pulled her into a hug, and Phoebe was grateful that, though she didn't know where her baby sister was, Halley had come back into her life.

A little while later, Phoebe was in the office catching up on paperwork. Because she hadn't planned to work, she was dressed casually in a pair of jeans and a fitted, sleeveless blouse. She spent an hour at her desk and on the computer before her stomach growled and she decided to grab a yogurt that she kept in the break room.

She leaned into the refrigerator, grabbed a container, and rose, bumping into Harvey as she stepped out of the way to close the appliance door. She never got the chance.

"Phoebe. I thought I saw you come in today." He didn't move from her personal space, and she shrank back into the cool, refrigerated air.

"I had paperwork to do." She tried to step around him, but he remained blocking her way.

"Those jeans fit you like a glove. I have to say, I like the look almost as much as those sexy suits you wear."

Disgust and panic warred for dominance. "I don't think that's appropriate for you to say to me," she told him, drawing back as far as she could go. So far, her ass was cold from the open fridge.

"Don't be a prude, Phoebe. I'm your boss. I can make life as nice as possible for you here or as unpleasant as I can. In other words, you scratch my back, I'll scratch yours."

Her anger rose at his audacity. "Here's the thing, Harvey. We're in the office. You keep this up, I'll scream and let half the staff come running to see what's wrong and you can scramble to cover your ass, or you can back off and leave me alone. I won't forget this happened but I won't make a scene. And I won't call your wife, either."

Although she deserved to know what a pig she was married to, chances are she wouldn't believe Phoebe anyway. She seemed completely happy to live the life he provided for her and bury her head in the sand about the man she was married to.

"I don't like your attitude, Phoebe. You don't have to work here, you know."

"No, I don't, but can you afford to lose me?" she asked, shaking inside but refusing to back down. "I'm consistently your top broker." God, she was so over this. "Move out of my way, Harvey." She tried to step around him, and this time he let her go.

Shaking, she headed for her desk, gathered her purse, and started for the door.

"Phoebe, are you okay?" Claudia asked as she rushed through the office.

"I'm okay," she said and walked into the warm summer air. She pulled in a deep breath, grateful to be outside and away from her boss.

God, the man had nerve, moving to overt sexual harassment. He had no shame and no concerns. She really didn't want to work here anymore. Could she open her own firm? She certainly had the reputation in this area as the broker to come to for high-end buyers and sellers.

She bit down on the inside of her cheek, knowing the time had come for her to make some serious decisions. In all aspects of her life.

BETWEEN MAJOR JOBS, Jake took the day off to get his new house in order. He was unpacking boxes in his house when the doorbell rang. Since he wasn't expecting visitors, he hoped like hell it wasn't another surprise by Lindsay. Instead he was shocked to open his door and find Halley Ward standing on his front porch.

Wearing a flowing dress and flip-flops, the complete opposite of what Phoebe would wear, she greeted him with a smile.

"Halley! What are you doing here?" He stepped aside and gestured for her to come in.

She strode past him and paused in the entryway. "I was hoping we could talk?"

Unsure of the nature of this visit, his nerves prickled uneasily. "Of course. I have an old couch we can sit on, but it's loaded up with boxes. Most of my new furniture still has to be delivered. Give me a second to make room."

She waved a hand. "Don't worry about it. We can stand."

"What's going on? Is Phoebe okay?" he asked, concerned.

"Well, she's going to kill me for coming here, so maybe we could keep this visit between us?"

He nodded. "Talk to me."

She bit down on her lower lip and nodded. "She came to see me earlier today. She's having a tough time sorting out past and present. And I know, because she told me, that you have no idea what's really going on inside her head. I just think you should know what she's thinking."

He frowned. "Normally I'd say I'd rather hear it from Phoebe, but clearly she's not going to tell me."

"No, because she's scared."

"Of what?" he asked, completely in the dark.

"She's scared of losing you again." Halley ran a hand through her hair and began pacing the floor as she explained. "You see, our mother abandoned us, she lost you, she saw the family she trusted turn you out. I'm sure she thought she was next."

He was confused. "But I'm back now."

Halley nodded. "And your ex-wife keeps showing up, threatening the status quo."

He blinked, stunned. "She thinks I'm going to go back to Lindsay?" He couldn't imagine Phoebe believing such a thing. Not after how close they'd gotten again.

"I think she's convinced herself that, somehow, Lindsay could come between you in the future. Or that life or fate will step in and take you away. It doesn't have to be rational. Emotions aren't. Trust me, I know. I pushed Kane away for my own reasons relating to my past and my fears."

He wasn't sure what to do with this information, how to use it to help him ease Phoebe's fears, but he was glad to have it. "Thanks for coming by. I appreciate you trying to help."

She smiled. "My pleasure."

He walked her out to her car and said good-bye, his mind on Phoebe and how he could convince her she was it for him. Now and forever. He knew the first step, and he planned to take care of it immediately.

Jake left his unpacked, unopened boxes and drove over to Master's Construction, where he knew he'd find Brent. He couldn't think of a more awkward conversation than the one he was about to have, but he couldn't see any way around it.

He entered the offices and walked to Brent's private area in the back, knocking on his door.

"Come in!" he called out.

Jake walked into the room, shutting the door behind him. "Hi. You busy?" he asked.

"Never too busy for you," Brent said. He gestured to the chairs across from his desk.

Jake took one, Brent sat in the other. "What can I do for you?" he asked.

Jake forced himself to meet the older man's gaze. If he was going to do this, he was going to man up about it. "It's about Lindsay."

"Aah. What did my headstrong daughter do now?" he asked, sounding resigned.

"Brent, you know this isn't easy. Putting you in the middle… it's not what I want to do. I just feel cornered. No matter how many times I make it clear to Lindsay that we're over and she has to move on, she doesn't hear me. I'm in the position of having to hurt her feelings over and over again, and it kills me."

Brent leaned on the arm of the chair, looking old and tired now. "I told her when she said she wanted to ask for a divorce so she could shake you up, that wasn't the right play to make. From that day on, she's been making wrong choices," he said, shaking his head.

"You know about my son, and I'm involved with his mother, and I can assure you that it changes nothing between me and Callie. However, Lindsay's not dealing with it well. Since she's not listening to me, I was hoping you could try having a talk with her. She keeps setting herself up to be hurt, and that's not something any of us wants."

"I'll take care of it, son. I want her to move on,

too. Be happy… find a good man to love."

Jake nodded, uncomfortable with the subject, but he'd started it. "Thank you."

He and Brent talked for a while about other things, personal and business, before Jake rose and headed out, his head clearer about the issues with his ex.

Now he could deal with Phoebe.

Chapter Eleven

PHOEBE DROPPED JAMIE off at a friend's house for dinner, then headed home for a meal of her own. She was in avoidance mode—avoiding work, preferring to research opening her own business, and avoiding Jake, claiming she had house showings in the evenings. She needed time and so she took some.

She'd already sat down with her aunt to discuss a business loan. There was Ward family money available, money handed down from generation to generation, and Aunt Joy wanted to give her the money as a gift, but Phoebe wanted to borrow and repay the loan without going to a bank or other lender. She had her pride and her business acumen and she would succeed. She just needed start-up money.

She was in the process of putting together a business plan, hadn't signed any agreements with Harvey preventing her from opening her own firm, and she wanted to get away from the perverted bastard as soon as possible. She'd hire new agents unless any at Harvey's firm came to her willingly. She wouldn't actively poach.

She was deep in thought and notes when her doorbell rang. She answered without looking through the window, something she'd lecture Jamie for doing and something she'd beat herself up for later.

"Hello, Lindsay. Jake's not here." And she'd already made it clear she didn't want to have anything to do with Phoebe. Although she had some nerve coming to Phoebe's house.

"Actually I'd like to speak to *you*." Lindsay shoved her hands into the front pockets of her jeans and rocked back and forth on her ballet-slipper shoes.

"Come in then." Phoebe waved her to come inside.

Lindsay shook her head. "No, thank you. I can say what I need to from here."

"Okay then." Phoebe leaned against the doorframe and waited.

"I want you to stay away from Jake."

Phoebe opened her mouth to speak, to tell her off, but Lindsay beat her to it.

"You have no idea what you've done, showing up like this. Before Jake saw you again, we were working our way back to each other." Her hands shook as she spoke, telling Phoebe she wasn't any more comfortable saying these things than Phoebe was hearing them.

Either that or she was lying.

Phoebe studied the other woman, who wasn't meeting her gaze. "My understanding is that you two have been over for years," Phoebe said. "In fact, you instigated the divorce. I'm not sure what kind of fantasy you've been building in your head but—"

"No fantasies. Jake is mine. Or he will be once you take yourself out of the picture."

Phoebe stiffened at the preposterous suggestion. "Why would I do that? Because you asked me to?"

"Because you're a mother and you know a little girl needs her father." Lindsay started up the steps, coming closer, begging as she spoke. "Especially one who grew up with him around. It's traumatizing for her to have her dad living apart from us."

Phoebe rolled her eyes. "Lindsay, you can't play me. You've been divorced for four years. Callie doesn't remember a time when you were living together, so *as a mother*, I suggest you stop using your daughter to get back a man who doesn't want you. He wants *me*." She pointed to herself. "He loves me."

Because she damn well loved him, and this woman wasn't taking him from her. Nor was Phoebe backing off so Lindsay could get her way. As Phoebe spoke, she became even more certain of words she hadn't even heard from his mouth. Yet. She sensed, because she hadn't given him an opening to say them. She'd kept him at arm's length, refusing to let him stay over, to become more of a family, because of her fears.

But with Lindsay here, putting her insecurities out there for Phoebe to hear, she realized how silly they were. Jake wasn't leaving her for Lindsay, not now and not in the future.

"He'll forget about you once he has his family back," Lindsay insisted. "And your son will have his father the way he's used to. As a part-time dad."

Phoebe blinked, struck by the fact that this woman really believed her own words. "Lindsay, if I were you, I would seriously look in the mirror and ask yourself if this behavior is what you want to teach your daughter. To run after a man who doesn't want you. How many times, in how many different ways, has Jake tried to tell you to back off? You just refuse to listen."

"You're wrong."

"And you're crazy if you think that, just because I left Jake, he'd come running back to you. He hasn't done it in four years. What makes you think he'd do it now? But none of that matters because I'm not going anywhere."

Lindsay looked stunned. As if she'd really believed Phoebe would do as she asked, and now that Phoebe had fought back, Lindsay didn't know what to do.

"Umm… good-bye?" Phoebe half asked, half said,

wanting to urge the other woman to leave.

Lindsay turned and walked back to her car, a sad woman who'd made her last stand.

Phoebe stared after her, stunned by the conversation but even more shaken by her own revelations. Courtesy of Lindsay, Phoebe realized she honestly, deep down believed Jake wouldn't leave her for any reason within his ability to control. Her past insecurities had to remain in the past or she'd lose the opportunity for the very future she wanted.

Her sister had said love was worth the risk but only Phoebe could convince herself to believe it, and she was right. They both had a mother who didn't know how to put the people she supposedly loved above all else, and Phoebe didn't want to be like her, mired in sadness, losing the people she loved. Nor did she want to set the wrong example for Jamie, that it was okay to run from your fears. Phoebe had been afraid to embrace the future, but when Lindsay had all but challenged her to step aside, she'd stepped up and claimed what was rightfully hers.

Now she had to tell the man himself that she was through running away.

❖ ❖ ❖

PHOEBE PULLED UP to Jake's house, nerves bouncing around in her stomach. She didn't know why she was so antsy. She knew how the man felt about her, but letting go of her reservations and going all in, giving him her heart… that was a big deal.

But it was long past time.

She rang the bell and didn't have too long to wait before he opened the door, shock registering on his face at the sight of her. In his faded jeans, hanging low on his hips, and a blue tee shirt that brought out the gorgeous color in his eyes, he was everything she wanted wrapped up in a sexy package.

Warm, caring, patient, hot, sexy, and a really good lover. She realized what a fool she was being worrying about a future she couldn't control when she could have now.

"Phoebe, hey!" A grin covered his face as he let her in. Instead of easing her nerves, the tempting smile amped her up even more. "I'm happy to see you," he said.

"I'm glad. Because the way I've been acting, I wouldn't have been surprised if you were annoyed with me."

He shook his head. "Never." He gave it some thought and said, "Well, maybe a little. You've been a bad girl, avoiding me," he said.

"Guilty." She rolled her shoulders, embarrassed at being figured out. "Can I explain why?"

"Only if you're ready." His expression softened as

he met her gaze, obviously aware this wasn't easy for her.

"I am." She'd already gathered her courage on the way over. "Past ready, and don't think your patience hasn't been noticed."

"I admit it was wearing thin." He grasped her elbow, and he led her to the old sofa, and they sat down across from each other.

She curled one leg beneath her and leaned in closer, his body heat and masculine scent making her aware of all she'd missed out on, keeping him at arm's length. "Can I say something before I get into the whole explanation?"

He nodded.

"I know I've been avoiding you lately, but the reasons have nothing to do with my feelings for you. Those have always been steady and sure, even when I haven't done a good enough job showing you how I feel."

"And how is that?" he asked in a gruff voice.

She braced her hands on either side of his handsome face, looking into his eyes. "I love you, Jake Nichols, and I think it's only right that I say it first. Because I've given you reason to doubt me."

He grasped on to her wrists, holding on to her and not letting her go. "Let's get one thing straight. I never doubted how you felt about me. I didn't understand your skittishness, but I felt in my heart you'd come around. And make no mistake, Phoebe Ward, I love you, too."

Her heart filled with warmth, hope, and happiness. "I knew that," she said, her smile wide. "I just didn't trust fate and life not to take you away from me again."

"I'm not going anywhere." He shifted, then pulled her into his arms so she was sitting across his lap. "And neither are you."

He kissed her, his lips sliding across hers in the most seductive, slow glide. Like they had all the time in the world—because they did. She moaned into his mouth, arching against him, trying to get as close as possible.

He slid a hand up the back of her shirt, rubbing in circles against her skin. "Can I ask what brought on the change of heart?"

"Let's just say I had a one-on-one conversation with your ex-wife, and in arguing with her, I did the convincing for myself."

He stiffened against her. "You had a run-in with Lindsay? Where?"

"At my house."

"I spoke to Brent about having a heart-to-heart with her. She should back off soon. I hope. Either way, I'm sorry you keep having to deal with her."

"She's part of your past. I can handle her. I realized we love each other and that's stronger than anything Lindsay throws at us." It was so simple. Once the words were out of her mouth, she'd realized she was behaving like the young girl afraid of losing family again instead of the woman invested in a good, trustworthy man. "Now can we stop talking about your ex and concentrate on us?"

She adjusted herself, straddling his lap and pulling his shirt off, tossing it onto the floor. As she reached for the button on his jeans, he shook his head.

"Not here." Standing with her in his arms, her legs wrapped around his waist, he walked her back to the bedroom. "We're going to christen my new bed."

She looped her arms around his neck, holding on tight. "My pleasure."

"It will be," he said, easing her down onto the bed.

She smiled, her eyes on the bulge in his jeans. Her sex softened, pulsing and wet, knowing how much he wanted her. "Strip, Jake." He grinned and did as she asked.

Soon he was naked and working on easing her denim down and off her legs. Together they removed the rest of her clothing and finally he came down on top of her, skin on skin at last.

She sighed at the feel of his hard, muscular body against her own. She needed to feel him moving, thick and hard inside her, of them joining together with no emotional walls between them.

He reached over to the bedside nightstand and returned with a foil packet in hand.

One she had no desire to use. "Jake? I'm on the pill," she said, her eyes on his face. "And I've never had sex without a condom."

"I'm clean. And if you're suggesting me, you, bare, I'm all in." He cupped his hand over her cheek and brought her face to his, kissing her with so much passion her heart burst inside her chest.

He eased up, bracing his arms on either side of her shoulders, grasped his cock in his hand, and set his hard erection against her core.

"Look at me when I enter you," he said, breaching her sex with one smooth thrust.

She moaned, squeezing her pussy around him, and he shuddered, his big body shaking with need. "You feel so good," he said in a rough voice. "And you want to know why?"

She arched, her nipples hardening, rubbing deliciously against his chest. "Why?" she practically purred.

"Because I love you," he said and began to move, driving into her over and over, the sweet sensations building immediately. With the friction of his skin against hers and no condom as a barrier, she felt every ridge and long, hard inch as he slowly, steadily made love to her. And when her climax hit, it rippled through her, encompassing all parts of her body, heart, and soul.

As she lay in his arms afterwards, relaxed and sated, she felt as if she could finally *breathe* after all these years.

JAKE SAT ON his deck at the end of summer. Phoebe brought a tray with plastic cups and lemonade in a pitcher, placing it on the outdoor table. Callie was on a swing hanging from the huge treated wood set Jake had installed in his backyard. Jamie pushed her on the swing like a good big brother until he got bored and moved on to throwing a baseball against a backboard with flexible netting.

"This is what I envisioned the first time I walked into the kitchen and looked out at this view," Jake said, glancing at his children, then the woman by his side.

She was more relaxed than he'd ever seen her. It had been one month since she'd told him she loved him. Almost the same amount of time since she'd quit her job and had begun preparations to open her own real estate company in Rosewood Bay. Being happy agreed with her.

Being more carefree did, as well. It helped that Brent's talk with Lindsay had accomplished its goal—that along with her confrontation with Phoebe. She'd actually apologized to them both for her behavior and had begun to make life easier when it came to him picking up Callie, and she'd stopped calling him for repairs she could hire someone to do.

He came up behind Phoebe and wrapped his arms around her waist. "Do you know how much I love you?"

"I should since you tell me every chance you get," she said, sounding content.

He'd given a lot of thought to what should happen next, especially in light of Kane's comments about waiting until Halley was ready for more. But Jake wasn't willing to wait for each step in his and Phoebe's relationship. He wanted her with him full time, and unlike Kane, he didn't want the whole family here when he asked.

"So I have a question for you." He kept one arm around her waist but reached into his front pocket with his other hand and pulled out a ring.

"Yes?" She leaned her head back against his shoulder for a brief moment.

"When I'm with you, wherever I'm with you, I have everything I want."

"Me, too," she whispered.

"Good. Then let's make it permanent and full time. Will you marry me?" he asked, holding out the ring for her to see.

"Jake!" She spun around in his arms. "Yes. Yes, I'll marry you."

He slipped the ring on her finger, and she kissed him long and hard until they heard voices.

"Dad!" This came from Jamie.

Jake knew the boy was used to seeing Jake kiss Phoebe.

"What's up?"

"Did you ask her?" Jamie wanted to know.

"Yeah, did you ask her?" Callie mimicked him.

Phoebe looked from the kids to Jake. "They know?"

He laughed. "I wanted Jamie's permission. And if I told one kid, I needed to tell the other. She said yes," he told them and was answered by resounding cheers.

Jake grinned. "Well, this is a"—he mentally can-celled out the word *damn* because of young ears—"really great day."

After years of being a screw-up, of thinking he had no future, he now looked around, realizing how damn lucky he was to have the family of his dreams. And the woman he would have waited a lifetime for.

Epilogue

WHAT COULD BE better than a wedding on the beach?

Phoebe stood at her sister's side as she married Kane on the stretch of beach behind her house. The ceremony was small and intimate, the bride barefoot in a wedding gown that draped her curves but very much suited Halley's Bohemian style, and Kane wore tuxedo pants, a white shirt, and bow tie.

Halley and Kane held hands as a justice of the peace married them.

Jamie and Nicky, his sister Andrea's son, stood by Kane's side, too. It was adorable.

She and Jake had decided to have a small wedding, as well. Although Jake was ready to run off and marry tomorrow, Phoebe did want her family surrounding her when she married the man she loved. And since this would be their first Christmas as a family, she wanted a December date.

Jake told her he'd wait forever if that's what it took. She didn't need forever. Just a winter wedding.

Phoebe took one last look at the people she loved before Halley and Kane were pronounced husband and wife. Her heart swelled at the sight of her family. One she'd never thought she would have, gathered together for this very happy occasion.

All that was missing was their baby sister, Juliette.

Next up in the Rosewood Bay series – Juliette's story.
Order FREED today!

Read on for an excerpt of FREED.

FREED

Fall for the missing Ward sister

Juliette Collins is privileged and isolated from the world by her over-protective father. She thinks she knows the truth about her history until a file on her father's computer reveals she has sisters she never knew about. A family she's never met. Betrayed, she realizes there's a life waiting for her outside the walls of her daddy's New York City penthouse and Juliet is determined to live it. Against her father's wishes, she heads to a small beach community to meet her siblings... and finds herself way out of her depth instead.

In the personal protection business, Braden Clark thinks nothing of taking on a job to watch over a city girl in town for the summer. If her father wants to know his daughter is safe, it's no problem and an easy way of earning a paycheck. Except Braden doesn't count on falling for the sheltered Juliette. Watching her experience her firsts, getting an apartment, finding a job, meeting up with her lost sisters, soon Braden's brand of protection becomes a little too personal. He's mixing business with pleasure and lying to a woman he's coming to care deeply about.

Sexual attraction burns bright between them and Braden is by her side as she finds herself, her family, and what it means to love... but what happens when she discovers his secret? That he's been paid to watch over her all along?

Order FREED today!

Chapter One

WHAT DO YOU buy the man who has everything for his birthday? Juliette Collins had discarded many idea gifts for her father, Andrew, and finally decided on purchasing a bottle of his favorite wine. He was the ultimate connoisseur and collector and had a wine cellar of his own. There was nothing else she could buy or surprise him with that he couldn't get for himself. At least this would be a personal present, showing him she knew him well and a gift he'd enjoy. But to order his favorite, she needed access to his wine journal, something he kept in his safe.

She handled his business dinners and social events, his doctor and other personal appointments, and coordinated with his assistant at his office, yet he hadn't shared the combination to his private safe. It was a good thing she'd spent hours as a child playing under his desk while he worked, sitting in a Queen Anne styled chair in the corner of the home office.

And when he went to his safe, he'd mutter the combination out loud, not knowing she paid attention. With her head for numbers, she'd memorized the combination years ago.

"Juliette," her father called, from across the penthouse where they lived, an immense space in Manhattan where she had her own wing.

"Yes?" She heard his footsteps making his way towards her bedroom.

As an investment banker, he often wined and dined his many wealthy clients. He also brought her along to chat with the wife or significant other while he handled more business type conversations during the meal. Tonight was one of those evenings, she thought, pasting a smile on her face, although she found the dinners and often the company, tedious. At least dinner out was preferable to the parties she hosted for him where too many of his so-called friends had grabby hands. Not that he knew. She was his princess and he'd be furious. She didn't see the point in upsetting him when she'd learned to deal with the too pushy men herself.

She was twenty-six. She'd been at his side since she turned eighteen, doing what he asked her whole life. She'd gone to New York University and majored in business, but instead of heading out into the world, as she'd been excited to do, her father's unexpected heart attack had kept her home, helping him, and feeding his overprotective nature. She ran his schedule now, including his cardiologist and cardiac rehab appointments because, despite his young age of fifty-two, he had a bad heart.

To say she was sheltered was an understatement. Her father, by virtue of his personality, took the term, helicopter parent, to the extreme. He held her back from living her life, claiming to need her by his side, and as he'd raised her since the death of her mother when she was an infant, and the doctors were concerned about his weak heart, she felt obligated to do as he asked. He was all she had… and vice versa.

He stepped into her room where she'd just finished getting ready for the day. Wearing his usual three-piece gray suit and a red tie, at fifty-two, he was a handsome, distinguished looking man, with salt and pepper hair and a goatee. His looks belied his actual state of health. His heart, after a quadruple bypass at forty-four and some damage from a heart attack, always worried her.

"What time is tonight's reservation at Chez Mathilde?" he asked.

"Seven o'clock and before you complain it's too early, the doctor said it was unhealthy for you to eat too late and go to bed on a full stomach, remember?"

He held out a hand, indicating he wouldn't argue.

"Yes and I appreciate you looking out for me. I don't know what I would do without you." He tended to throw that last line on most conversations, a way of reminding her how much he needed her.

She adored him. Sometimes she just wanted ... more than she had in her life now. "Are you leaving for the office?" she asked him.

He nodded. "I'll be back home in time to rest before dinner."

"Have a good day."

He strode over and kissed the top of her head. "You too. What are you doing today?"

"I'll come by the office and coordinate with Georgia," she said of his assistant. "Then I'll probably do some shopping."

"Take my driver. I'll send Eric back after he takes me to the office."

She shook her head. "I can take the subway."

She caught his scowl. "You know I don't think it's safe."

"Then I'll walk for a bit, get some fresh air, and grab a cab. I don't need—"

"Humor me, please? I don't want to worry about you." His hand went to his chest. "Eric will be here for you by the time you're ready to leave."

She sighed. "Fine," she said, giving in as she always did.

"I'll see you later." He strode out of her room.

She watched him go, struck by how easily he manipulated her, and she let him.

She wasn't about to second-guess the choices she made in her life. It was what it was. He was her only parent, she loved him, and she felt as if she needed to take care of him. Included in that care was keeping him calm about her own life.

She waited a while until she was certain he'd left for work, and she headed into his home office. The dark paneled room had black leather furnishings, including the Queen Anne, a love seat and the chair behind his desk. The office always had a welcoming feel to it. That and it smelled of her father. Since she was a little girl, she associated that scent with home and found it comforting.

She walked to the safe, located behind a painting, a cliché if ever there was one, and spun the dial—He'd never upgraded to a more modern numerical touch keypad—and let herself into the safe. The dark space forced her to pull out the contents for viewing in order to search for the one she wanted with the listing of his wines.

There were folders on top and leather-bound journals underneath. She shifted the folders, which were identified by typeset labels and caught sight of her name. Curious, she placed the other items onto a table and flipped through the folder to see what was inside.

A private investigator's report.

Subjects: Phoebe and Halley Ward, females ages 18 and 20.

Another page. Subject: Meg Ward Gifford.

Juliette froze. Meg Ward was her mother's name. She continued reading, gleaning quite the education on the parent she'd thought was dead.

The woman she'd believed her father had loved so unconditionally there hadn't been another female for him since. Instead, Juliette was reading that the woman had sold drugs, been incarcerated, and lost two children to foster care. The report had been updated periodically over the years. The sisters lived in a beach town in Connecticut called Rosewood Bay, and Meg—her mother—lived in a city not far from there.

If Meg had other children, that meant Juliette had... sisters. Legs shaking, she lowered herself to the nearest chair, reeling from the news.

Her mother was alive?

She had siblings?

Her father had lied to her all these years?

Betrayal rippled through her. Her father, the one she'd given up her life for and trusted unconditionaly, had been keeping the mother of all secrets, pun intended.

She didn't know where to begin to sort through

her emotions. Shock, for sure. Anger at her father, for certain. And a growing sense of excitement over the fact that she had family.

For years, it had been just Juliette and her father. Lonely but at least she'd had one parent and he'd loved her in his own suffocating way. But to have sisters? Grown women who shared her blood, who were out there. Did they know about her? According to the report they'd been young when they'd entered foster care. Ages six and three. Juliette had obviously ended up with her father before they'd gone into the system or she might have wound up there, as well.

She bit down on her lower lip, thinking. Wondering why her father had withheld this information from her? Why not tell her the truth about her mother? Her sisters? Hadn't she deserved to know? Had he really taken his overprotectiveness this far? Or was there another reason he'd kept her in the dark?

She spent the day nursing her anger, not taking the walk she'd planned, and definitely skipping the trip to her father's office.

Instead, she researched her own family on the internet. Phoebe was a realtor in Rosewood Bay, Halley an artist, a painter who had showings in New York City. So close, Juliette thought, and she'd had no idea.

Tears formed in her eyes as she took in the pictures of her sisters on the screen. The three of them looked nothing alike, but the more she read about them, the more her heart filled, and she suddenly realized what that empty feeling in her life had been about all these years. The hole in her heart was where her sisters should have been.

She waited until her father came home, meeting him in his office where he always stopped first.

He placed his briefcase down onto his desk before turning to her. "Juliette. You didn't come into the office today. Are you feeling all right?" he asked, sounding concerned.

She straightened her shoulders in preparation for the upcoming confrontation. "I'd like an explanation," she said, holding out the folder she'd been reading and rereading all day. The papers trembled in her hands.

He stared at the sheaths, shock on his face. "What were you doing in my safe?"

That was his concern? "Looking for your wine journal so I could buy you a birthday gift." She shook the folder at him. "Tell me something that makes sense. Give me a reason you'd tell me that my mother was dead?" she asked, her voice rising.

He swallowed hard, his throat moving up and down, but she had to give him credit, he didn't flinch. "Would you have rather I told you she was a drug addict?" he asked. "Because that's what she is."

"Yes, considering it was the truth."

He met her gaze, no remorse in his eyes or expression. "I was protecting you from life's harsher realities."

And there it was. The reason she'd feared. Over protectiveness was the cause for basing her life on a lie. "You weren't doing me any favors. I had a right to know. Was my mother a drug addict when you met her?" she asked, desperate for more information about the parent she'd never known.

He shrugged, lifting his shoulders. "I don't know. She didn't seem to be at the time. We met at a bar I had gone to after a business dinner. She was there having drinks with a friend. One thing led to another... We got together a few times afterwards."

"So she got pregnant by accident," Juliette murmured, making an obvious assumption.

"She saw a mark," he said with a shake of his head, eyes narrowing, his gaze hard, the change taking her by surprise. "I never thought to discuss this with you, but if you must know, she supplied the birth control. I realized when she came to me for money because she was pregnant, she must have planned it, to the extent one can plan such things. A desperate woman poking holes in a condom. Or at the very least, if it was an accident, she wasn't disappointed because she'd figured out by then I had money."

She didn't want to think through the specifics of

her father's sex life.

"But the fact is," he went on. "She was a calculating bitch." His voice was like ice.

She'd seen him this cold before, when things didn't go his way in business, or when she fought him too hard to get her own way. Even so, she shivered at the toneless way he spoke to her, as if this weren't her past, her life, her mother he was discussing but an inconvenience that annoyed him.

"I paid her for a while but when I realized you weren't in the kind of home you deserved. I made it worth her while to give you to me and go away. And I won't apologize for protecting you from her ever since."

Tears welled in her eyes at how he was missing the point. That it was all based on lies. "What about my sisters?" she asked. "You just left them with her?"

"They weren't my children," he said simply.

"So you walked away even though you just said she wasn't fit to raise *me*?"

"I met her when I was twenty-six and building my career. I took you, had to hire a nanny, to change my life. There wasn't anything I could have done for them. As I'm sure you read, the state ultimately stepped in and took them away. I'm sure they were better off."

It was such a stark, brutal reality. The kind he'd

been protecting her from for years, as he'd said. The irony was, he'd also protected her from the knowledge that he was just as cold as her mother apparently was.

Juliette turned away, wiping the tears away. "What about once I was an adult? Why didn't you tell me I had sisters?"

"Because for all I knew, they're no different than your mother."

She spun back to face him, horrified by that statement. "I looked them up. You had them investigated. You know they're accomplished women. You just wanted to keep me for yourself." Locked away in this ivory tower, taking care of him and not living her own life, making her own decisions.

"You've had a good life, haven't you, Juliette?" he asked, his voice softening. "You and I? Together?"

His question just cemented the truth she'd just come to accept. She realized now the extent of his selfishness. Because he'd gotten sick when she was eighteen, she'd let herself believe he truly needed her but the fact was he just wanted her around. She had no doubt he loved her but his brand of love wasn't healthy.

"You had no right to keep the truth from me," she said. "None." Without another word, she turned around and walked out of the room.

Juliette didn't sleep that night. She tossed and

turned, thinking of the fact that she had a family out there she didn't know. Her mother, well, there was every chance Juliette wouldn't want to know her but her sisters? Her heart leapt at the chance to meet the two women, to find them, to have a family beyond her father and the walls of this penthouse.

By the time the sun came up, shining into her room, she knew what she had to do. Rosewood Bay was waiting for her and with it, the sisters she longed to know and just maybe a brand new life.

She took her time over the next few days, planning her next move. She had a difficult time finding an apartment in Rosewood Bay because summer rentals were all taken, as it was late June. But she managed to find a one bedroom furnished apartment in town. It sounded small but she didn't care. She rented it sight unseen. She wanted to get a job, too. She didn't think her father would cut her off but if she was going to make a stand, she might as well go all the way and be a self-sufficient adult. She'd worry about what kind of job when she got there.

She was packing the things she needed in her suitcase when her father knocked on her door.

"Come in." She didn't stop what she was doing, folding her summer dresses and placing them in the open luggage.

"What are you doing?" The first hint of true panic

since he'd been found out sliced into her father's voice.

"I'm leaving."

He rushed over, placing a hand on her suitcase. "Juliette, no. We can work this out. I want to make this right."

"You can't." The damage was done by withholding information about her family.

"Be reasonable before you storm out. You've never been away from home alone. Never held a job. What are your plans?"

"And whose fault is that? You've kept me dependent on you but now it's time for me to be an adult. To meet my sisters and live my own life." She closed her suitcase and zipped it around before turning to face him. "I can promise you, I will be perfectly fine."

"I only ever had your best interest at heart. You have to know that." He stepped back, a defeated expression on his face. "Would you consider taking a bodyguard?" he asked. "Someone to watch you from afar?"

She snorted at that. "No. I'm an adult and it's time you started treating me like one. I'm taking the summer for myself. I'll decide what happens at the end of August. Until then, please respect my privacy."

He hesitated, then perhaps seeing the determination in her expression, the certainty about her decision in her voice, he lifted a hand and stepped back. "Fine. I'll expect to hear from you. Often."

She shook her head. "Sorry, dad. You're not telling me what to do anymore." She hesitated, knowing he had a bad heart and not wanting to upset him more despite how hurt and angry she was. "I know you love me," she said, voice softening. "And I love you, but it's way past time for me to be on my own."

"So be it."

She narrowed her gaze, surprised at his capitulation. She'd expected him to turn his chilly anger on her but he was letting her go without too much of an argument.

Relief and excitement filled her soul. She was going to meet her family, experience everything she'd missed out on and finally, live her own life.

For herself and nobody else.

LEGS UP ON his desk, Braden Clark disconnected the call he'd been on, surprised at the lengths some people would go to in order to maintain control of the people in their lives. But if Andrew Collins, New York City investment banker wanted him to keep tabs on his daughter who was coming to Rosewood Bay for the summer, Braden figured it was a job.

A damn good-paying one, he thought, thinking of

the number he'd quoted the man and how easily he'd agreed. It required hands-on work, which prevented him from handling something else at the same time, so it was only fair.

"New job?" Mike Graham, his best friend and new partner asked from his seat at the desk across from Braden's.

Braden had taken over Clark Investigations from his dad, who'd had to retire due to his recent Alzheimer's diagnosis. Braden had returned a year ago when his dad had started showing signs of forgetfulness, leaving his job with the NYC police department to come home. Needing a change of pace, Mike had come along and bought into the company, which was now known as Clark and Graham Investigations. This new case had come in as a referral from a Manhattan P.I. Braden knew from his days on the force.

"New and *cushy* job," Braden replied to his partner's question. "Keeping an eye on some rich guy's daughter for the summer."

"How old is she? Under eighteen? That ought to be fun, hanging out at the cheap bars in town. Better you than me," he said, chuckling.

At thirty, they preferred the more upscale Blue Wall restaurant and bar to the cheaper kid hangouts closer to the beach.

Braden shook his head. "She's more like twenty-six

years old."

Mike's eyes widened. "And daddy's still keeping tabs? Spoiled little rich girl coming to the beach for the summer?" he guessed.

"Sounded like it. Sheltered and first time out on her own." He shrugged. "Doesn't seem like a difficult assignment."

"Unless she's a troll." Mike smirked at the possibility.

"He's sending a photo." Braden pulled up his laptop and checked his email. "Yep. Here it is." He clicked to open the picture and sucked in a breath at the sight of the woman in the photo.

"That bad?" Mike asked.

"That good." Braden let out a low whistle, feeling the kick in his gut again as he looked at the beautiful woman on the screen.

Light brown hair, porcelain skin and a delicate profile that took his breath away. She wore a tiara in the photo, obviously a picture from a party of some sort, and she looked every inch the princess from a fairy tale.

His cock, dormant and he thought, immune to women since his ex did her damage, stiffened behind his jeans.

Well, damn.

"You going to show me?" Mike asked.

Braden felt suddenly possessive of the photo and the woman in it. Reluctantly, he turned the screen towards his friend.

Mike let out an appreciative whistle. "Damn, you're going to have a fucking fun summer."

Braden scowled at him. "You know she's a job and that means hands off."

Mike tilted his head back and laughed hard. "Yeah, good luck with that."

His friend had a point. Just looking at the woman had his cock hard and ready. Ignoring the obvious attraction on paper wasn't going to be easy when he saw her in person. Still, he was a professional.

He could handle the job. And the woman.

"How's things with your dad?" Mike asked, changing the subject to one Braden really didn't want to discuss. But his friend meant well and nothing could alter the painful reality that was his father's life. *His* life.

Still, Mike meant well by asking. "He's holding steady. He can still be alone with Mrs. Mulligan next door looking out for him while I'm out."

Mike nodded. "Good. I hope it stays that way for a while. It'll be tough to have to consider nursing homes." He nodded to the stack of pamphlets on Braden's desk.

Braden had been looking into places so he'd be

prepared when the time came. He just hoped to postpone the decision as long as possible. And it would be his choice, which hurt his heart.

He'd been an only child growing up and had been close to his dad. He'd appreciated not having to share the father-son moments, the trips they'd taken, the games they'd played. Except now, as an adult, he understood the value of siblings. Of sharing the burdens. His mom was gone ten years now and dealing with his father's illness and care was all on him.

And that was all he wanted to dwell on his problems. He'd rather focus on work.

His gaze zeroed back on the laptop screen and the more pleasurable part of his life, the job he had coming up. He'd have to find Ms. Juliette Collins in Rosewood Bay. Despite the influx of summer visitors, it shouldn't be hard for him to locate someone new looking to find a job in town and fit in. Newcomers usually stood out.

And with looks like hers, he'd at least enjoy the view for the summer, even if he had to keep his hands to himself.

Order FREED today!

About the Author

Carly Phillips is the *N.Y. Times* and *USA Today* Best-selling Author of over 50 sexy contemporary romance novels featuring hot men, strong women and the emotionally compelling stories her readers have come to expect and love. Carly's career spans over a decade and a half with various New York publishing houses, and she is now an Indie author who runs her own business and loves every exciting minute of her publishing journey. Carly is happily married to her college sweetheart, the mother of two nearly adult daughters and three crazy dogs (two wheaten terriers and one mutant Havanese) who star on her Facebook Fan Page and website. Carly loves social media and is always around to interact with her readers.

Keep up with Carly and her upcoming books:

Website:
www.carlyphillips.com

Sign up for Carly's Newsletter:
www.carlyphillips.com/newsletter-sign-up

Carly on Facebook:
facebook.com/CarlyPhillipsFanPage

Carly on Twitter:
twitter.com/carlyphillips

Hang out at Carly's Corner! (Hot guys & giveaways!)
smarturl.it/CarlysCornerFB

76121510R00141

Made in the USA
Middletown, DE
10 June 2018